Dead Words

And More Weird Stories

by

Donald J. Gavron

Copyright © Donald J. Gavron, 2017

PUBLISHER'S NOTE
This is a work of fiction. Names, characters, places
and incidents are either the product of the author's
imagination or are used fictitiously, and any
resemblance to actual persons, living or dead,
business establishments, events or locales is entirely
coincidental. No part of this book may be used or
reproduced without written permission except in the
case of brief quotations embodied in critical articles
and reviews.

ISBN-13: 978-1544905587
ISBN-10: 1544905580

Printed in the United States of America

Cover design & art © Donald J. Gavron, 2017

for Anna

CONTENTS

My Affair with the Hadron Collider

It all starts with a wink, a smile, and a lecture on disambiguation. Physics was never a passion of mine. In fact, I was always a passionless person. I tried not to let things interfere with my thought processes. Maybe that's why I lived alone above a deli and worked in a Shell station.

Certain things do catch my attention, and the lecture on the Large Hadron Collider (LHC) at the Guggenheim Museum drew my interest. Particle physicist Michael Tuts was giving the lecture, broadcast from Geneva, and I bought a ticket for the February 6th event.

I was not disappointed. The lecture posed the ultimate question: Why do we exist? The LHC was the world's largest particle accelerator, and it held the answers to a multitude of questions. It was a scientific oracle, a time machine, and a goddess of love. In two hours I had reached a state of euphoria that threatened to send me into paroxysms of joy. The origin of mass, space and time were all within our grasp. The composition of the universe became clear. I had come to the conclusion that inside the LHC was God. And I would get inside the LHC.

It was a thing of beauty. Solidly constructed. All the tubes and pipes coming together in some sort of majestic highway leading into the depths of matrix mechanics. It had a purity and symmetry that was unmatched, and I could understand how physicists lost their souls in their research.

Beneath the Franco-Swiss border was a tunnel 17 miles in circumference. Inside the tunnel, 574 feet below the ground, was my true love, my universal soul, the Large Hadron Collider. Getting inside was another matter (no pun intended).

After the lecture I read everything I could on the LHC, including the purported existence of the Higgs boson. I had decided that the Higgs bosun was my competition for the love of the LHC, and it was my duty to destroy it (and other false theories), even though its existence had yet to be confirmed.

I learned that the universe consisted of 23% dark matter. String theory advanced the notion of alternate universes. Do all known particles have super symmetric partners? According to the lecture, and my research, each fermion should have a partner bosun. It all sounded very romantic to me, more compelling than Keats and Shelley.

Emptying my bank account (and borrowing money from the deli owner) I booked a flight to Geneva, to be near my newfound love.

I sat back in my seat on the airplane. Man-made particle collisions were taking place, and I wanted to be a part of it. I wanted to collide with the Hadron Collider and gain all the secrets of the universe.

I fell asleep, and dreamed of sleptons, photinos and squarks. It was a great deal to absorb.

After the plane landed I felt rejuvenated, full of purpose. I wasn't ever going back stateside. In fact, I vowed to never visit a deli or a gas station again. The past is the past.

I got a cheap hotel room (above a coffee shop) and plotted my course of action. Money would be difficult, but I was resourceful.

In a few days I got a job sweeping the streets and washing dishes. I eventually moved to a small room above an abattoir. I continued to read about high-energy physics, ions, muons, J/ψ meson and Upsilon particles, quark-gluon plasma; and ALICE, which stood for A Large Ion Collider Experiment. ALICE became my dream of dreams, my wonderland, and my plan was to reach through the looking glass to meet her. Again, I was smitten. But after a while, I fell back to the Hadron Collider, my first true love. ALICE would have to wait.

Three years later, I am still here, plotting and planning, reading and absorbing, sweeping and washing, waiting for the right time to confront my desire. It was all coming into focus. They say unrequited love is the purest love. So I wait, and preserve the dream.

Dead Words

I was employed by a lawyer for most of the first decade of the new century. He specialized in the disposition of the possessions of those clients who passed from this earth without benefit of relative or executor. The lawyer in question, my employer, Mr. Thomas Alva Quinn, was well versed in his legal domain. Nevertheless, it remained a mystery to me for quite some time as to how he could secure the right to do what he did, and hence make a substantial living from it. At the time I had no desire to analyze the situation. I needed a job (as many did during the reign of the W.), and when the Employment Office sent me to Quinn, I was not inclined to turn him down.

Quinn was, to put it mildly, an eccentric. He was unmarried and lived a good portion of his life with his widowed mother, who passed on two years before I entered his employ. To my knowledge he did not pursue either female or male companionship, and showed no interest in anything of a sexual nature. He had two true passions, connected symbiotically by vocation and avocation. Circumventing his way through the legal labyrinth was his vocation. The acquisition of the weird and the obscure was his avocation.

His job fueled his passion for collecting. One did not exist without the other. He had no other vices that I could ascertain. He neither smoked nor drank, and what he ate every day would not satisfy a normal person. At 50 years, he was twice my age, yet he strained to give himself the appearance of a peer to me, and I did nothing to dissuade him from his acting endeavors.

I waited diligently for him at my apartment at the YMCA. A call would come for me downstairs at the desk and I would make haste to receive it. Quinn would simply give me a time and a place (he avoided details over the phone), and I would usually have ample passage to prepare myself to do his bidding. Two or three days, sometimes a week would pass before I was needed after his call, but I had best be ready when he demanded. One day I was half an hour late and I can tell you that after Quinn's tirade I was never late again. He paid me well and regularly, and I was in good conscience able to overlook his quixotic behavior. I did not say much around Quinn; I was content simply to observe, and I imagine he thought me retarded, or slow. The long scar on my forehead from a childhood injury must have convinced him that I was a botched lobotomy case, and I must confess I took pleasure in deluding him that I was dim-witted.

I did some light administrative work, some heavy lifting, renting of trucks and equipment. He taught me his computer invoice system, the most rudimentary of skills, but I was not privy to his list of locked folders, protected by his secret code.

Quinn, as I stated before, was legally entitled to dispose of his dead clients' belongings, and once they made their entrance to the void, he was banging on the door with a key or a crowbar to dispose of their wares. A great deal of material was given to charity, which Quinn wrote off, of course. More than several antiques found their way into local museums. Money, bonds, keys to vaults were kept and the outcome never mentioned.

There were the rare coin collections, first editions by famous authors, jewelry, paintings, precious sculptures, and assorted keepsakes. But it was the peculiar that brought his life into focus. Some of the oddities he came across were extreme in the least, and these bizarre discoveries he often shared with me.

There were old medical photo collections of people in various states of decay belonging to an ex-doctor who was trying to find a vaccine for leprosy. There was the tattooed skin taken from the arm of a courtesan's husband, preserved under glass some 30 years after his death. The cane made of bone honed from the owner's amputated, gangrenous leg. The dead stuffed cat collection. The remnants of things inhuman swimming in alcohol-filled mason jars. The 30 shrunken heads discovered by the war veteran in a cave in the Philippines. Then, finally, there were the cremated remains of loved ones found in urns, shoe polish containers and zip-lock bags. Some of these things made me ill, but exhilarated, and after a while I grew immune to these weird belongings.

Quinn kept most of the things of value, except for one particular type of item, something that he had no interest in whatsoever, and I understood why — They were the journals, the diaries and the letters he instructed me to burn, the very things that became my fascination. Quinn had no desire to learn about the thoughts of the dead clients whose pockets he picked. He would prefer to size them up by their penchant for the bizarre. This was his way of preserving his sanity. Look at the dried umbilical cords preserved in Lucite, the dog's skull, and the insect collection — He would point them out to me. He would reduce the people who owned them, label them crazy, and then rationalize his ripping them off. The words interested me, the words left by the dead. It was the only record anyone was likely to see beyond the surface possessions, which so often defined the deceased. I was eager to learn about the hopes and dreams of these people who were once vibrant, alive, and walking the earth. The idea of a window into another person's soul became my obsession, and I pursed this with a passion I could find for nothing else.

So, I became a collector of dead people's words; journals of despair; letters of heartache; diaries of disappointment, regret and sadness. I knew reading them that I was not alone. Threads of anxiety wove their way through my rapidly growing collection, a collection I kept secret from Quinn. Who knows what he would do to me if he found out? But it was like a dangerous drug I could not kick, and it was encompassing my life slowly, inexorably. I began to look forward to our plunders. They became my *raison d'être.*

Soon eight years passed, during which the country turned to ruin. Quinn's business inexplicably thrived however. The circus of life continued and I drifted more inward, becoming more and more reclusive, like Quinn, watching the parade go by. What cared I for others and the workings of the world? The world was a screwed up place before I was born and it will be screwed up long after I am dead and gone. All that mattered to me at that time were the journals and the dead words.

Some of the diaries were long, near Dickensian records covering years of marriage, divorce, childbirth, death, lust and romantic disillusionment. One woman wrote of her involvement with a married man and went into every sexual detail imaginable, some even beyond my imagination. These passages I saved for cold and lonely nights. One man wrote of his war experience in Vietnam. It ended abruptly days before the Tet offensive. The diary was found with his belongings at his base and sent home to his parents, who wrapped it neatly in plastic, burying it at the bottom of the son's toy chest, the one his father built for him when he was five years old. Some entries I felt should be preserved, and I hoped to show them to others once my career with Quinn ended, but as long as he was alive I dared not speak of them, as their existence was contrary to his instruction.

Some of the journals went nowhere, and were even without name. Can you imagine endeavoring to keep a record of your life, no matter how narrow or obscure, without revealing the name of the author to the world? The thought escaped me.

When I wasn't working for Quinn, I had several temp jobs that never managed to branch out into much of anything. A data entry office only called me when another employee was sick and the office was desperate. The other job was separating machine parts in a storage warehouse. That paid better, but they called me even more infrequently than the data entry job. So, I had little choice but to stay with Quinn.

My room at the Y cost $180 a month and I cannot tell you how many times I had to put the touch on Quinn for a few dollars to help me make the rent. I ate at several diners in (and on the outskirts of) town, rotating between them so as not to appear a low-life yearning for a home-cooked meal. The library was next to the Y and I made use of the stacks every day. I read the news, leafed through the magazines and occasionally checked out a book, preferably a novel that I usually did not finish. I never bothered with bios or nonfiction; their claims of authenticity seemed specious and transparent. It was, after all, one person's final judgment on another's life, an author's attempt at omniscience, at being God.

The words I collected did not seem tainted with that arrogance. They were sincere. Moreover, they were more alive to me than anyone walking the street. They became my friends, and I did not judge them.

****

It was a cold day in November and the furnace at the Y was not working. The staff was all set to move us to a shelter, but I refused to go. I spent a few days in one a short time after my parents died, and it was not pleasant. None of my relatives would have me, preferring to believe the innuendo surrounding me instead of their own flesh and blood, and I have severed ties with them all since then.

In any event, I was robbed and beaten in the shelter and spent a few days in the hospital. There a kindly social worker named Sonja helped find for me my current dwelling at the Y. Suffice it to say I was not keen on the idea of spending another night in a shelter.

I gathered a few belongings and some of my precious diaries and letters to look over, and proceeded to a neighborhood bar. The bar was cold and dark. Was this lack of heat a community wide thing?

I had several shots of whiskey and a beer, hoping to summon some courage to call Quinn and see if he could put me up. Just then, a tall blonde woman with thin legs sat on the stool next to me, shoving a cigarette into my face. Light, she said. I obliged her.

She began to talk in a tough, husky-throated voice. I couldn't stop her. She had on a short red skirt, and once she crossed her legs the skirt moved tightly up her thighs. She accidentally kicked my bag, placed on the floor between our stools, and I suddenly became suspicious of this person. She had black circles under her eyes and her hands were large with protruding veins. Her nails looked false, pasted on.

As I reached down to check my bag she crossed her legs again and I noticed a bulge in the crotch area of "her" dress. I grabbed my bag and fled, almost forgetting to pay the tab.

I walked and walked, putting as much distance between the bar and myself as possible. Snowflakes began to fall, but they looked more like ash from the textile plant down the road. All the buildings I passed seemed deserted.

I came to a phone booth and decided to call Quinn, unable to delay my anxiety a second longer. The phone rang for what seemed an eternity, with no answering machine to pick up.

Finally, the ringing stopped, and a voice broke through the void. Quinn seemed calm and unburdened, more than willing to help. He was going away for a few days, but he was sympathetic to my plight. There was a house clearing probate, near the waterfront, and I was welcome to stay there, providing there was no "monkey business."

"I know you," he said, "you're not into wild nights and such." And he was right. He knew I would not do anything out of the ordinary, but he had to remind me anyway. Sensing that he might have misspoken, Quinn shifted gears and invited me to dine with him, before showing me the house. I gladly accepted. I was down to my last $5 and the 99¢ cheeseburger special ended yesterday.

We met at an old diner near the bridge leading to Staten Island and Quinn told me that I could have anything I wanted. I did not want to disappoint his generosity, ordering glazed ham, garlic mashed potatoes, corn on the cob, fries with gravy, iced tea, and a large vanilla shake. Quinn drank coffee, black, and patiently waited for me to finish. I was his audience, and he began to pontificate.

"This house, it's a big house. I can only let you stay there for a few days, you understand, but you will have heat and electricity, so it will not be uncomfortable. Just don't turn too many lights on. Noisy neighbors and all. The people who owned it died a few weeks ago. The husband poisoned himself and his wife."

He paused, letting me soak this in, knowing that it would affect me.

"While you're there I want you to check the place out, do some preliminary inventory for me, just in case something goes wrong. This new judge is a real stickler for details and I do not want anything valuable to be left there too long. You're a smart kid. You know what to do."

Yes, I was smart, smart enough to see through his condescending opinion of me. I had nowhere else to go and for me this meant that I was again unable to control my own destiny. I vowed to one day be free of Quinn, to make something of my life, to find my place in the world. On this night, however, I needed sleep and warmth, so I succumbed to Quinn's offer.

The house was near the waterfront, on a street above but within view of the bay. Quinn explained to me that during the 1930s and '40s that this was the prime vacation arena for the rich and strange and that many of the houses dated back to the turn of the century. We drove to a house on a corner lot near a cemetery; one that Quinn apprised me was also of historical importance. Gigantic hedges surrounded the front lawn of the house; twin granite lions were placed on either side of the stone stairway leading to the front door. The house itself was white with a black-shingled roof. Iron bars protected the windows and the house looked ancient, like a fortress hidden from society. I didn't feel frightened. I had been into enough dwellings with Quinn alone to know that there was nothing to fear except the workings of the mind. Dead was dead, as Quinn liked to say. He gave me the key and reminded me again of my duties, then drove off in his silver BMW into the tree-shrouded night.

I walked up the stairs, the wind rustling the vines growing along the concrete base of the house. The two imposing lion statues flanking the steps sat there with majestic melancholy, as if waiting for some long dead master to return.

I entered a side door and turned on my flashlight, searching for a light switch or lamp. I was mindful of what Quinn said about too many lights and the neighbors being nosy, but no one cared, really. I doubted that the police would have to be called. If they were, I would simply explain that Quinn let me sleep there, I was his assistant, etc.

There was a tiny lamp on a marble end table, and I reached over and turned it on. It seemed to illuminate the entire room — a vast cavernous parlor whose every inch was filled with clutter, old pictures, dust and more dust. I was not afraid in the least; in fact, I welcomed this opportunity to cut myself off from the world for a while.

It always helped me to find a nice comfortable hole to crawl into, at least until the world stopped being so frighteningly cruel, and I could tolerate it again. I never bought the old "think positive" mantra. I tried to see the world for what it was — A vast jungle plain, a killing ground disguised as the emerald city, a wasteland from coast to coast. People were so predictable, for the most part, except for the few odd dreamers, the ones who never fit in, even with the outsiders. The people I got to know from my dead word collection were the closest I ever got to human friendship. It suited me fine. I got to know them and I could still hide myself from their judgments, as surely judgments they would have if they met me.

The couch was huge, plump and inviting, and seemed like a nice place to settle down for the night. I did not feel like meddling with the bedrooms upstairs, as I am sure that is where the foul deed took place.

One thing bothered me, though. If the husband did murder his wife and commit suicide, why was there no remnant of a police investigation? Was Quinn trying to scare me? This could not be beyond reason.

Quinn was an enigma, and a parasite. I could feel the life being sucked out of me when I was in his presence and, after all these years, it finally sunk in. I would rest, get a good night's rest, and then I would leave, and leave him for good. I would go to California, travel along the coast to Big Sur, settle in some fishing village and remain anonymous for the balance of my life.

But now I needed sleep in the worst way; I was so tired I was almost drunk with haziness. I opened some shades and the moonlight cast some half-light through the yellow-stained windows, giving me enough brightness to convince me that I was not going to sleep in a coffin.

I took off my work boots and my jacket and lay down on the vast purple sofa, my bag filled with letters and journals at my side. I was even too tired to read them, as I did most every night. My mind raced, though, as my body fell off into listless decay. I could not slow the pace of my brain, thinking, analyzing, and mournfully dreaming.

My eyes closed and time melted away. I drifted into a near-fluid state of sleep approaching consciousness, but not quite breaking through the surface.

A noise beckoned me from the darkness of sleep, tapping like a hammer against the thin veil of my cocoon. I opened my eyes, light from the moonlit street creeping in through the windows. My eyes scanned the room and everything began to become clear in the darkness, like a negative being developed slowly in a photo lab.

I looked at the furniture and the high-backed velour cushioned chairs straight from some 1920s salon. It seemed as if the vague outline in the chair was more than a cushion or a doubled over blanket. It resembled a statue or something more tangible, more fluid, more alive.

Trying to read my watch, I brought my hand up to my face. The watch face was missing; it was a blank orb, shiny, numberless. When I brought my hand down, a pair of eyes, tiny and glowing like moonlight, stared back at me from the darkness. I wanted to leap up from the couch, but I felt powerless. Nothing was holding me down that I could feel. It was as if a dense consciousness was sitting on my chest.

There were more eyes, more figures, now rising from their perches around the room. All the while the tap, tap, tap of what was probably a telephone wire rapping against the house, the shadows from the trees casting wild forms against the windows, dancing with a mad fury that could only signal a storm approaching, all conspired to disrupt my mind.

I was not afraid, surprisingly, even as the figures approached me, the eyes glistening, surrounding me, my body paralyzed as if I were given a spinal anesthetic. Then, the voices came forward, each in their turn, carefully impassioned speeches uttered with the most confident elocution.

"My name is Ingrid Sawyer. I worked on a farm for my entire life. My father took me from school to tend to the animals and to help my mother. That's what they did in those days. I wrote it all down. You read it. I had no friends, except for my diary. My father didn't want me to read, but my mother taught me. I wrote in my book, but he found it, found out I was writing about boys, Jimmy Swanson mostly. I saw him at the carnival. I tried to get him to notice me, but he didn't. My father found out I was writing about him and he was afraid I would run away, so he took the diary away from me and hid it, and I never found it. I never even wrote my name in it."

"I am called Miguel Sant'Angelo. As a student, my teacher, Miss Townsend, taught me English. Years later, I sent her letters and she agreed to meet me. I was 18 and she was 10 years older than I was. Our affair started slowly, like a flower unfolding in the spring. Her parents disapproved of me because I was foreign, but we continued to see each other. Then, she moved away. I confronted her parents and they said that she had married a wealthy man who wanted children. I tried to contact her. I continued to send her letters, but I do not know if she ever got them."

"My name's Tommy Ashbery, PFC, second platoon, third squad. I wrote to my parents every day during my tour, mostly about the ordinary boring events leading up to the battle that took my life. I tried to make things sound normal, but in truth, they weren't. I lied to keep them happy, so that they wouldn't worry that I would possibly lose my life. I was their only son and it would be devastating to them. I wished that even after I was killed someone would continue to write to them to pretend to be me so that they wouldn't worry. Even though I never came back, he could invent a life and convince them I was happy and this would curb their sadness that I was never coming home alive."

They declared themselves, one after another, the people, the dead people who wrote the journals, letters, and diaries that I had kept. They were all here in the room, staring at me, speaking to me, it seemed all at once, but I could understand them all clearly. The voices turned into a cacophony, a humming wave of noise that saturated the room, beneath it all the tap, tap, tap of the wire against the side of the house. Then they began to ask me questions.

"Who put you up to this? What made you think that you could read our innermost thoughts? These are our words. Who said you could read them? Why have you come to us, summoned us? Why don't you let us rest and morbidly attaching yourself to our dreams?"

They moved closer, and for the first time I began to tremble, or was allowed by the force that held me captive to tremble. Still, I could not move enough to escape my prone position on the couch. I glanced around. The purple velour of the couch took on the shape of a coffin, with myself tucked neatly into the middle as the glistening eyes of the dead souls I had intruded upon held on to the sides and rocked me gently ever gently into a submissive form of sleep.

****

I awoke on what must have been a sweaty sheet of ice, the tapping of the wire burning into the veins in my forehead, daylight flooding the room with dusty strewn rays. I leapt from the couch and looked at it. It was just an ordinary couch. The room was empty. The bag was still on the floor. I leaned over cautiously, slowly, not knowing what I would find. Gone. Gone. Back to their respective owners? Or did I lose them somewhere along the way?

My nerves were ragged, but I felt energized. I gathered my bag, a few books and some clothes. With finality, I elected to leave this life and Quinn and all the ghosts of my past in my wake.

My new chance was short-lived, however, as the police tightened the net on Quinn and gathered me in with him the next day. A few days later I was interrogated and only after many exhaustive hours of discussion did I learn that they had suspected me and Quinn of killing the people he had represented and helping ourselves to the spoils left after their demise.

I thought they would charge me, but after I told them of my theft of the words and the visitation I received from their owners, my candor appeared to placate them enough that I was sentenced to a psychiatric hospital.

Quinn would later confess, and he was given life in a penitentiary upstate. Not all the tabloid notoriety appealed to him, and he hanged himself just a few short weeks into his incarceration.

I felt sorry for him in a slight way and wondered if he was ever visited by any of the entities I encountered.

In some strange way, never being completely cleared of suspicion somehow worked to my advantage. I spent six months in the psychiatric hospital and when I was released I sold my story to a magazine.

Later, a German publishing company offered me a substantial sum to elaborate on my life and psychic experiences. The offer to publish was too good to pass up. I was no writer, but they said they would put me in touch with someone who could distill my experiences. A ghostwriter, someone chuckled.

I took the money and bought a house by a lake. I spend my time fishing and thinking now, but sometimes the ghosts visit me. Sometimes I am in an old bookstore, and I see the diaries there. In one dream, I opened one and it was blank. I thought their secrets were safe, and when they came to me in my dreams I told them this.

The stories I told the ghostwriter were part true, part made up, but now I do not know the difference, or if that ever mattered.

Ladybug

I was eating lunch with my friend Bill at Dunkin' Donuts. We were talking about the creation of the universe and he seemed to have some interesting ideas, which he presented forcefully and sincerely. Bill mentioned King Solomon, the Initiates, Hitler and a Golden Wire. I had no idea where he was going with all this claptrap.

"Look," I said, interrupting him. "We can never know what we don't know. You can't conceive of infinity, so you can't explain God or the Universe." He looked at me quizzically.

"There's something on your shoulder," he said, pointing. I turned my neck and saw what appeared to be a fly on my shirt. I flicked it off and it landed on the floor.

"It's a ladybug," he said. "Also known as coccinella septempunctata." He lifted it up off the ground and placed it on the table.

"Damn, I hope I didn't kill it."

"No. It's moving."

I looked at its red, black-spotted shell and noticed two protuberances from its back, coming from under the shell.

"What are those things?" I said.

"Wings."

"Why are they sticking out like that? Did I hurt them?" I was concerned. "They're supposed to be good luck. I hope I didn't..."

"It's all right. And even if it's not all right it's all written. Maybe it lived its time."

I was going through a bad phase in my life and I didn't need any worse luck. I didn't want the killing of a ladybug on my conscience.

"You know ladybugs are directly descended from the Virgin Mary," Bill said, back on his horse. I considered this. Now I was worried that I'd killed a descendant of Jesus' mom.

We sat and talked and watched the ladybug move around. Bill was an artist, a painter, and some of his work was being exhibited in a library nearby. He was someone who struggled through life, trying to find order and acceptance. But he was also prone to conspiracy theories, cult indoctrination, and a frequent willingness to blame everyone else for his troubles. We had gone through some similar experiences in life. He liked music and books, and we listened to each other like lost souls on a deserted island. But at some point he had gone off the rails. My friend talked and drew diagrams on his note pad, again attempting to explain the workings of the universe to me. I watched the wings on the ladybug, and after a while they slowly retracted. My friend talked and I listened to his crazy theories, but the ladybug was on my mind. We finished eating. The bug had stopped moving.

"Maybe it's dead."

"Maybe it was meant to be. A friend of mine tried to rescue a butterfly from a spider's web once. He accidentally pulled one of the wings off. Maybe it was just time for it to die. It served its purpose here."

No. I wasn't about to accept that. Not as far as this ladybug was concerned. I poked at it gently. It was still alive. I slid a packet of sugar under it and lifted it from the table. I carried it like a wounded bird cupped in my palms as we went outside. My friend waved to me and went to his car.

"Peace, brother," he said.

I walked over to a tiny island of grass and shrubs in the parking lot, across the way from a building that was just being demolished, a building that once housed a store that was built just last year. I looked around at one of the shrubs for a place to drop the ladybug and noticed a huge spider web. I sure wasn't going to put it there, not after that story about the butterfly my friend told me, so I brought the bug into my car and placed it in my cup holder. I was going to drive it home with me and find a spot for it somewhere. I kept looking over at it from time to time to make sure it was all right. I turned the radio off so the noise wouldn't disturb it. On the way, we stopped at a real estate agent's office to find the ladybug an apartment. There were a few openings in the area, but every one she took us to had spider webs in the rooms.

"I can't take any of these," I said, infuriated, and we left, the ladybug still clinging to the sugar packet.

We finally arrived at my condo. I tried coaxing the ladybug off the sugar packet and onto a shrub near my front porch. But I'll be damned if the shrub didn't have a spider web on it. So, I took the ladybug in and maneuvered it into a small plastic cup with some ferns and blades of grass and placed it near my sink. I crumbled up some angel food cake and tossed it in the cup. It seemed to be happy there, and my guilt that I had harmed it disappeared.

I remembered something else my friend Bill said. "No, we don't come back as bugs, or cats, or cows. We elevate to the Divine Spirit, but only if you are IN TUNE with it."

A few days later the ladybug hanged itself with a piece of dental floss. I guess it was depressed. I did everything I could think of and it still died. Maybe I didn't pay enough attention to it. I had no answer that would give me solace. "Maybe it was time" did not give me closure. Frantic, I tried to call my friend but a message said his phone was disconnected. I was never able to contact him again.

The Man with the Mask on the Bridge

Have you ever told someone to "go jump off a bridge," whether in anger or jest? Or have you ever thought of taking a leap yourself? Keep this in mind when you consider the story I am about to tell you.

In the books and magazines I've been reading lately — usually ones I pick up in the doctor's office or at the airport — there's a character that is disaffected (a term we used to call "alienated" during the 70s) and the guy (usually it's a guy) is undergoing some kind of personal crisis. He feels askew, his head is clouded, he's in a daze and he's having trouble with reality. The character is either an architect, a bank teller or a rich guy who's having a psychological rift that would make Kafka's ear stand on end. In each case the guy is at his wit's end. The writer sends him through the loops and then leaves him (and the reader) hanging. It's left up to us (the reader) to decide if the guy is crazy, sane, or just some allegorical misfit. There is no explanation for all this. It is just there for all to be amazed at, wrapped in ads for body fragrance, custom suits, imported cigars and whiskies.

I must say I don't like these stories. I prefer that there be some resolution, the protagonist coming to some epiphany or realization concerning man, God or whatever the fuck's bothering him, and let that be that. I have no patience for these stories, but I read them. They pass the time. It's all right if the main character, the protagonist (as my English Lit teacher called him) suffered some displacement, some "alienation," as long as a resolution was achieved, a point. He can be shown dealing with the complexities of the world, its mysteries, its contradictions, but the reader (as my teacher said) must achieve an "aesthetic stasis," — a calm, analytical appreciation of the dilemma. Kafka's bug story is one such tale. We feel for his plight even though we know he did not turn into a bug, but he thought he did (as least I think so) and this illustrated (without going into too much detail) his family problem(s). It's better if the protagonist finds his/her way through their psychic dilemma, finds a way to live his/her life in response to the fantastic plight experienced. They find a way to wade through the murk and go on (as Beckett says). So much for stasis. I say all of this because I have my own story to tell, and it is every bit as perplexing to me as all the others I have ever read, whether they are believable or formulaic. What I am about to tell you is true, to the best of my knowledge; whether my memory can be trusted is open to interpretation.

I was driving home, at 5:45 p.m., Friday the 13th, when I received a call about a jumper. I was already having a bad day and looking forward to opening a bottle of wine, cooking a steak, and relaxing, maybe watching a Cary Grant movie that was on TCM that night.

Everything changed with the call. I attempted to compartmentalize all my problems and face the moment at hand (just as they taught us in Stress Class 101 and on the motivational tapes I purchased).

The dispatcher gave me the raw details over the car phone.

"Jumper. Age unknown. On the Victory Bridge over Raritan Bay. Fire Department's been alerted. The bridge is being blocked. Do you copy?"

"I copy. I'm on my way."

The bridge mentioned was due to be demolished. It was built in the thirties, an old web of steel, a relic that would be torn down to make way for a concrete structure twice as tall and nowhere near as adroit in character. I used to drag race over the Victory Bridge when I was in High School. The sound of the tires on the grated latticework that covered the bridge's span was something that stayed in your memory bank; the sound of air being pushed through the metal grates gave me a feeling of flying, of immortality.

"One more thing," the dispatcher said.

"Yes?"

"The guy's wearing some kind of what looks like a mask or costume. Copy?"

I paused for a moment. I was less than one minute away. I could see the flashing red and blue lights from around the corner.

"Copy that. What kind of mask? Like a stocking mask, a surgical mask?"

"Like Halloween. We don't know for sure yet."

"What else is he wearing?"

"Jeans. Black shoes or sneakers. Black jacket."

"Is that all?"

"That's all we know. It's going to turn into a goddamn circus real quick. We need you there pronto!"

"I'm here," and as I said it I was.

I parked my car behind a phalanx of patrol cars. I saw several officers standing around, looking up. One saw me and pointed at the apex of the bridge's arm where the figure was located. I walked up to the officer that looked the least perplexed. We talked in short hand. He gave me a walkie-talkie, nodded and twitched his head. "Good luck. Go get 'em."

That's what I do. I go and get them. That's my job. There are only a few people specifically trained to interact with jumpers in our department. They don't want someone untrained (like the normal beat officer) doing something to spark the guy to jump. That's only common sense. In my eighteen years on the force I've dealt with eighty-four jumpers. There were many more you just don't get a chance to save. They park the car on the top of the bridge and get out and jump, like they're late for an appointment, or they're too embarrassed that someone will see them; or they just don't want to take the chance that somebody will talk them out of it. It happens a lot more than you think. Eight of the ones I did get a chance to speak to were women I managed to talk down. Most of the time they only just want to talk or be heard. They were abused, or pregnant and didn't want to have the kid, they were conflicted, depressed, on drugs, pills, etc. They have their say and then they come down. One brief moment of insanity. One desperate cry for help. Most of them do come down. Six of the ones I talked to did not. One guy stayed on the ledge of a bank for six hours before he caved. Four left notes behind. When you leave a note it's like signing a contract. You'd look foolish if you didn't do it. All the bodies were recovered except for one, who jumped into the river. I knew all the names of the guys who jumped by heart. The ones who didn't I forgot. It's funny. They were all men. In all but one case I met the guy's family (because he didn't have one), if only to explain how sorry I was. It's the hardest thing to do. To say I'm giving them closure would be insincere. There is no closure. One guy's father made me understand that. He told me I didn't do enough, and I agreed. Most of the time the wives understood; they could see it coming; they were prepared. One guy had three kids under ten years old. I check back on some of the family members when I'm able to. My analyst tells me I must let go, but I can't.

I started to climb up the catwalk. I have a belt attached to the steel cable that slides along until I get to a cross section of cable, then I detach it and move it across the bump where the cables intersect and I move on. I do this about a dozen times. I take it slow. I approached with caution, clearing my throat, making some noise. I didn't want to scare him into falling. I wanted him to know right off the bat who I was and why I was there.

When I get close enough I start to jabber.

"How ya doin'? Coming up. Take it slow," I say, any such nonsense just to fill the dead air. I get as close as I can before I sense that he's uncomfortable. I'm about thirty feet away, staring up. I stop. Not too close.

"Cold up here," I say. No answer. His back is to me, but he hears me. Black windbreaker, just like the dispatcher said. Dirty sneakers, high tops, and old. The jeans are dark blue and appear new, stiff. He's wearing gloves, black leather gloves. No skin is visible so I can't see if he's white, dark, African-American, Latino, whatever. I couldn't tell how old he was, anything. Not yet. The fact that he had not decided to jump gave me hope. As I said, these people usually just want to talk.

"What's going on, brother? Something botherin' you?"

He turns around. Then I see the mask. It startles me at first. He wants it to. It's a skull with a black dome, a chalk white face with dark crevices like sculptured bones sticking through mummified skin. It's rubber and it moves as he breathes, like it has merged with the skin. There are holes for the eyes and a slit for the mouth, but I can't see his eyes or mouth, just dark portholes to a disturbed soul.

"No. Go away," he says in a stern, muffled monotone. No trace of an accent.

"Anything I can do?" I keep asking questions. If he keeps answering I know I'm getting somewhere.

"Okay. I hear you." That's one of the first things you say. They want to be heard. "Can you tell me what you're doing way up here?"

"Good a place as any. Not bothering anyone."

Right now, I want to ask him if he's going to jump, but I can't. This might spark him. My communicator's on and they can hear me on the ground. They talk back and only I can hear. There's a psychiatrist, a doctor and probably now a lawyer all listening in. I must walk a fine line. It's a game plan you must follow. If I feel that he's serious I can punch a code into the 2-way that will let them know. I don't know if he's serious yet. The mask tells me he wants a circus; he's looking for attention. Whether he wants to take a dive as a grand finale is anyone's guess. The wind is picking up. It makes its own unintelligible cry.

With jumpers, it's all speculation. You're in a realm that is completely unknown. You try to narrow it down in segments by asking questions — but that only leads to more questions. It's like trying to navigate a sailboat through a hurricane.

Guys like this one like to create a scene. They crave the attention. They need an audience, either to witness the deed or to be talked down and cheered to as they are taken away. See their name in the paper.

"What's your name?" I ask. Another question. A big one. I've learned the hard way that if they tell you their name, then you know they want to be talked down.

"I don't have one." So much for that.

"What should I call you?" I'm fishing for something, anything.

"I don't have one." You see how this works. It's a game, like poker or chess.

"Can I get you something?" I give you something, you give me something. Give a pawn, take a pawn.

"No. Not now. Not now."

"Maybe later then? Coffee? Cigarette?"

"Don't smoke. Don't drink coffee."

"There must be something you want."

"Yeah, I want to be fucking left alone," he blurts out. I pause for a while to let the anger die off.

"Is there someone you'd like us to notify? A wife? Girl? Parents?"

"That's for me to know."

"And for me to find out? So, what do you want to talk about?"

"Who says I want to talk about anything? Who invited you anyway? I'm just up here admiring the view."

The mask. The voice modulating throughout the rubber, smothered by the rubber. It was getting to me. One second it was red, like a devil's mask; then it was gray like a skull. I still couldn't tell anything through the slits. The mask covered his head completely. He has a scarf wrapped around his throat and a black skintight shirt. There was also a black hood that he tried to cover his head with, but the wind kept blowing it back. He was a shadow with a mask on a bridge.

He was probably young. I guessed fewer than thirty. I wasn't picking up on anything else.

"It must be hard to breathe with that thing on."

"What thing?"

"That ... that mask."

"What mask? ... It must be hard to breathe with that thing that you have on," he said mockingly. I forced myself to laugh, but my teeth started to chatter.

"What's that?" I asked, playing along, hoping he'd play a card I could pick up and use.

"Your skin."

"Indeed it is."

"Indeed it is," he said, mocking me again.

I looked around. Heights don't bother me very much. I'm aware of the risks, even with the safety belt. The thing is not to sacrifice your safety at the expense of the jumper. If you do that then you're both going over.

"So, what brings you here?"

"Like I said: the view."

"It's a little cold. If you want to admire the skyline we can go downtown. It's much safer."

"Looking out a window with bars on it?"

"No. I never said that."

"I like it here. I like to be as close to the elements as possible."

"Isn't it cold?"

"I don't think so."

There was a pause of about ten seconds that felt like ten minutes. The cold breeze picked up and whipped around. His hood blew off again. He braced himself with his legs and used both hands to grab it and cover his head. I thought that: if I got closer, and this happened I could possibly make a grab for him. But he was fast. I would have to table that thought.

"Does your wife know where you are?" I ask.

"You mean: If I had one?"

"You have any kids?"

"I told you: No... I used to."

Now I was getting somewhere. This could lead in a hundred different directions (if he was telling the truth). His kid or kids could have died, been taken away, any number of things. I had to narrow it down."

"How old are they?" I said, presuming them to be alive.

"Do you have any?" he said in that gray modulated tone, turning the tables on me.

"No. I have a nephew and a niece. They're great kids."

"Kids change everything."

"That's what everyone says. My nephew lived with us for a few years after his mother died. He's a great kid. Sixteen now..."

"It's not the same thing as your own."

"I suppose not. But I love him nonetheless."

"There's nothing to suppose."

"What do you have: Boy? Girl?"

No response. He was looking away, at the horizon. It was starting to get grayer, colder. We both watched the light fading away. Then he said something unexpected.

"It's like God turning a dimmer switch, isn't it?"

"Do you believe in God?"

"Do you?"

"I'd better," I said, looking down at the flashing lights on the bridge. "Or I wouldn't be up here."

He started to laugh, in a low register that began to vibrate into a contralto. I noticed the color of the mask changed to a dark crimson. Or had it always been that way?

"You're a funny guy. You have a name?" he asked.

"It's Greg. Greg Notches."

"What kind of name is that?"

"My father was Portuguese. At least his parents were. My mother was Irish."

"Any other cops in the family?"

"No. I'm the only one."

The breeze picked up again. The mask now seemed to ripple with the wind. Again, it seemed to adhere to his skin like a living thing, a second face. I was getting a little dizzy. I don't know why.

Suddenly my 2-way radio was buzzing with static.

"You better take that," the man with the mask said. "It might be your mother."

"My mother's dead," I wanted to reply, but didn't. He was starting to annoy me. His condescending remarks, his pseudo-poetic take on his situation — it all was piling up. I almost wished he would jump.

"This is Greg," I said into the radio.

There was nothing but static. It was going right through my head. I noticed a sizable crowd had gathered on the ground. Ambulances, fire trucks and police cars all stood ready. Yellow tape blocked off the crowd, the witnesses in waiting praying for a high dive into the river below. The PAFD was trying to rig a net. Didn't they have anything else to do with their lives?

"You know what happens when your dreams die?" he asked, out of the blue. He said this with a modicum of resignation, his flippant nature put aside for a moment. I pretended not to hear, trying to find out if this was indeed an opening or just another petulant remark.

"I'm sorry. You were saying...?" Force him out.

"Don't be sorry. I said: Dreams. I was talking about dreams."

"What about dreams?"

"I mean dreams when you're a kid, a young man; things like that. Not the type of dreams you have when you're asleep."

"I know what you mean."

"Dead. All my dreams are dead. Gone." He was off in thought. I had to try and stabilize him, bring him back to some rational state.

"So, you know my name. What should I call you?"

"Nat."

"Nat? Is that short for Nathaniel?"

"No. It's short for Gnat. Like the bug."

And that was all he was prepared to give me.

He grew more somber, his head hanging, his shoulders drooping. I sensed that he was stiffening up, getting ready to jump, but he didn't. It was the mask. The mask was almost too much for me to handle. It was affecting me in a way I didn't know how to deal with. The man with the mask was under my skin, like a tic or a super virus. Suffice it to say, I never had to deal with a situation like this before. A fucking guy with a fucking mask. It was too weird to be true. I was cold, hungry, and I had problems of my own to attend to. I almost wished the motherfucker would jump. Jump or come down; either way it made little difference at this point as long as this charade was over fast.

My phone flashed green. That meant that they wanted to talk to me. Yellow meant come down, regardless of the situation. Red meant they were coming up, but to stay up. I couldn't talk now, or didn't want to. Then the light started flashing yellow. But I wasn't coming down either. I felt that if I did the man in the mask would jump. My mind was in a kind of limbo state. Suddenly I felt responsible for him in some strange way. Dusk was settling across the bay. The wind was steady, with strong gusts at infrequent intervals. It was now just over half an hour since I made the climb to talk to the man with the mask. At this point, after half an hour, many of them jumped. The longer they took, the more chance I had of talking him down. This was a good sign.

Just then two officers in heavy flak jackets and ear mufflers came into view, climbing in our direction.

"Company," The mask said, nodding his demonic face.

"Go back," I yelled in my command voice. "I'm in charge here."

"The Captain said..."

"I don't give a shit. Get back down. You want this guy on your conscience?"

"Yeah, get a conscience," the mask said.

I turned around to face him. The mask grinned at me.

"Please," was all I said. I turned back.

"I mean it. No one else." I turned on my two-way. "Captain get these clowns off my back." He asked me if I was making progress.

"Yes. Yes, I am," I said, lying through my chattering teeth. "He's serious."

I brought the walkie-talkie to my chest, holding it like a valuable artifact.

"My Captain wants to know if you need anything?"

"Pizza. Double pepperoni." I repeated that into the mic. "It would be easier if you come down, he says. We can get a table at Sciortino's." I smiled. The mask moved through a series of contortions, the cheekbones appeared to stretch the face muscles and were tinted a shade of green. The more I looked at him, the less and less it appeared to me a mask. It was more like a living thing going through some metamorphosis on his face, a separate living organism. I shook my head. How could that be possible? Was I losing my mind?

"No. Bring it up."

"I'll be in touch, chief." I hung up and shut the unit off, hooking it to my belt. "He's going to see about the double pepperoni."

"Good."

"I'm getting hungry myself."

"Well, this is almost over."

"Oh? Really? I wish we had more time to talk."

"Well, your Captain, he's concerned. That's why he called. Either shit or get off the pot, right?"

"No, that's not it. We're here for you, Nat. Whatever you need."

"My name's not Nat."

"Okay. I thought so. Can you tell me your real name? Is there anything I can do for you?"

"I need a new life. Can you get me that?"

"People start over all the time."

"How about you? Have you ever had to start over?"

I paused to make sure my words had sufficient weight."

"Yes. Every day."

"Oh, you're one of those 'one-day-at-a-time' fellows."

"Not really."

"You drink?"

"Not much. Sometimes. Yes. Tonight, I'll be having a few."

And he laughed. The mask shivered with his laughter. Then he moved his hands along the railing a few feet away from me. He turned his head. The rays of the setting sun marked the contours of his face with deep shadows. I saw the glint of an eyeball in one of the crevices, a bright sliver like a diamond's glare. The mask was baked on his face, irremovable, unalterable except perhaps by a beam of light directed at it, and the bellowing wind.

"You're having trouble with your wife," he said, like a bolt of lightning. This was all getting to be too much.

"How do you know?" I was done being careful with him. The gloves were about to come off.

"Your daughter died a long time ago."

"How the hell would you know that?" He was right. How the hell did he know?

"I guessed." His expression was blank. The mask was like a solid rock. I took a few seconds to pull myself together. Focus.

"You must have been thorough something similar."

"What could be as bad?"

"Lots of things," I said, my voice drained of meaning. "What you're going through must be pretty bad to lead you to this."

"Chin up, Greg. You're a man who has been through hell and back and yet you're up here trying to talk me down. Me. A total stranger. Let me tell you something. No matter what you say or do I am going to jump off this bridge. As soon as the last rays of that sun disappear I am off. But, we have some unfinished business, you and me."

"What do you mean?"

"Why don't you go down? I'll wait until you get all the way down and then I'll jump. They told you to come down, didn't they?"

"They did."

"So, go."

"I can't. It's my job."

"You've done your job. No one can argue that."

"I have to stay. It's my responsibility."

"You're trying to give me a guilt complex, Greg. It's all hazard. Life is just an arbitrary set of circumstances. Look at what happened to you today. You never thought you'd wind up here. You were on your way home. Yet, here you are."

"You seem like an intelligent guy. We can talk some more. We can work our whatever it is that's bothering you."

"I doubt it. My choice. Freedom of choice. No offense, old man, but you can't even help yourself."

"Everyone has problems."

"Call your Captain. Tell him you're coming down."

"I'm not!" I was just as adamant in not coming down as he appeared to be about jumping.

"Look, if I delay my exit ... if I tell you what's bothering me, why I've made this decision ... what led me to this situation ... then will you leave me alone?"

"I have to hear what you have to say first."

"You drive a hard bargain, Greg. I guess that's why you're a negotiator."

"I'm here to listen."

He paused. Hands on the rail, leaning back, swaying back and forth as if he was on a playground swing. Then he stopped and looked directly at me, trying to hypnotize me, and the face came to life again.

"Look at that horizon. Have you ever witnessed anything so beautiful? Peaceful. Calm. If only that was the only thing to it."

"When you remove yourself from everything it gets better. If I was in that city another day it would take all my willpower not to cut my throat. How can people live like that? Constant stress. How can they make it through the day? Worrying about how to make money for other people while you yourself starve. Go to school. Get a job. Work for a corporation. Learn all the buzzwords. Get married. Have a kid or three. Bury yourself in debt and then spend the rest of your life trying to climb out from under it all. Is it worth it? Is it? You can't go anywhere nowadays without some asshole getting a cell phone call. You're in the movies. Everybody's texting. You're in a bookstore in the poetry section reading Pablo Neruda and there's some dweeb on the other side of the rack talking into space about his hernia operation. You're in a urinal and there's some guy cursing somebody else out, calling him a motherfucker. There's no peace anymore. No privacy. They should confiscate all the cell phones and round up all their rude owners and destroy them."

"Is that it? Cell phones?"

"I had a passion once. I dreamed the dream. Then ten, twenty years go by, and you wonder if you've been wasting your time, living someone else's dream of who you should be. You wonder if you should have bought more lottery tickets.

"You wake up one day and you realize it's all a fraud. You've been living a lie. The entire fabric of your being has been false. Lying to yourself: that's the greatest sin. If you believe in sin.

"Once you realize your life is a sham, people start to act differently towards you. They think you're a loser. Even the therapist you're seeing thinks so too. You have a wife and kids and she meets someone else and she leaves. Then your kids must grow up with half a father. The other half is the boyfriend, the lover, and the other husband. Maybe they call him 'dad' behind your back.

"You don't realize until it's too late that you love her, or once did but not enough. You bring flowers but it's too late. You took everything for granted. Then the job doesn't make sense anymore. The food you eat has no taste. Other things happen. Minor things that seem like the end of the world. The garbage bag breaks. The cable goes out. Someone keys in the wrong payment on a bill and you must talk to sixteen different people to straighten it all out. No one understands you. You yell at someone at work. You get fired. No one understands what you're going through. Suddenly you're forty years old and you have no wife, no kids, no family, no job, no career, and no dreams. There is no peace, no solace. Only death to look forward to. A calmness. A peace. Something to stop the pounding in your head. And that's it. You wind up on a bridge. And you make a choice."

"You have to come down," I said. I was drained. The last vestiges of the sun were hanging on the far horizon. My teeth were cold. "We can talk some more. I understand. Believe me. We can work this out."

"No one cares. Do I look like I want to spend the rest of my life in a rubber room with someone shining a flashlight in my eyes to make sure I'm not catatonic?"

"We're all in the same boat."

"But some of us are in first class. Some of us have life jackets. Some are in the hold rowing like crazy with hash marks on their backs."

"Life isn't fair. A lot of people are dealt an unfair hand."

"That doesn't make me feel any better."

"Sometimes things get better."

"Is that what you believe, Greg?"

"Yes, I have to."

"Are you sure you're not fooling yourself?"

"I'm still here. We're in the same place."

"And you tell me you haven't thought about jumping? Honestly? Be honest for once in your life."

"Maybe I have." I bowed my head. How could he have seen through me so clearly? The railing was ice cold, like a dinosaur bone. The cold went right to the soles of my feet. I didn't think it was possible to feel any colder. Icy pricks like freezing needles penetrated my skin. My fingers were numb.

His cloak spread out now like a giant set of wings, flapping haphazardly in the wind. A strong gust might fling him off the side. I felt pity for him now, but that did not assuage my desire to see him jump, to get it over, to end the pain. I gave up. I didn't know how to get to him. In a few minutes I would have to go back. If I did, how could I face my colleagues again?

"Is that what happened to Baker?"

"What?"

"You gave up. You gave up on Baker, didn't you?"

"John Baker?"

"You know who I'm talking about."

Night was wrapping its slow cloak around us. The lights from the bridge and the boats in the harbor and the cityscape and the pale moon were our only beacons.

"What about Willowicz? McCoy? Standowski? Jiminez? You didn't speak Spanish well enough or you might have helped. Since then you learned. But it hasn't brought him back."

He recited the names of all the men who jumped that I tried to talk down. The ones I failed to help.

"Who are you?" I said with resignation.

"I just told you who I am: Baker. Willowicz. McCoy. Standowski. Jimenez. Stanton. And Williams. Williams was the worst, wasn't it?"

Sgt. Ben Williams. My partner for eleven years. He had terminal cancer.

"Nothing you could do about him, right, Mr. Do-Gooder? You tell yourself SIX, but it's really SEVEN."

"How do you know? Who the fuck are you?" I yell, letting my rage take over.

"Maybe they're better off. Maybe you didn't fail them, Greg."

Maybe it was me on the ledge. The cold made me imagine myself looking out from the mask. Maybe my mind was playing tricks on me like the characters in a Chuck Palahniuk novel, or some other cheap paperback. I was cold, so bitter cold. Numb and yet wide awake. Just my imagination, like that Rolling Stones song.

"You have to answer. Not for these men. They've made their choices. The things you must answer for are your own self-centeredness, your sense of importance. What makes you feel that you and you alone can talk them down?"

"The same people who think they can fight fires. The same people that teach that think they can teach..."

"So, you're a teacher now?"

"They don't necessarily think they're better than..."

"They do. They all do. And what are you?"

"I'm ... a reasonable man."

"You have a grip on things?"

The mask had veins. It was hideous now. Pulsating.

"I'm holding on. Every day."

"That's right. Every day."

He laughed. He was mocking me. He had nothing else to do but try to humiliate himself through me.

"Why do you do what you do?"

"Someone has to," I say. And with that he jumped into the dark abyss of night. The cloak fluttered for a second or two and I thought he was going to fly away, but that was all a figment.

He didn't fly away. He fell. As he passed the lights from the parapet below I saw his body miss the concrete stations by a few feet and crash into the water below with a thunderclap. He quickly disappeared from my view.

I was leaning over the railing. I felt light-headed. The desire to jump was there with me, as it was with all the ones I failed to save. Baker, Willowicz. McCoy. Standowski. Jiménez. Stanton. Even Williams.

One hand at a time, carefully, I made my way down to safety. I was still dizzy, but by force of will I composed myself. The figures and lights below became vague, out of focus, but I still inched my way down. I could hear Captain Cullen's voice.

"... Nowhere to be found ... not a trace ... Coast Guard called out ... what went on up there?"

As soon as I took my last step to the concrete sidewalk below I fainted. The next thing I knew I was in the hospital, talking to Jolene, my dispatcher at the precinct.

******

I took a leave of absence. I went back to the bridge a few weeks later. I didn't know what I expected to find. By coincidence it was near dusk, the same time in the evening I began my encounter with the jumper.

I looked at the bridge, slated for demolition later in the year. The steel swing-bridge resembled the skeleton of some old dinosaur from the land of the lost. It was a huge empty shell enveloping me as I walked across it. But it had a sort of majestic presence, a solidity, and a watchful solemnity.

I did feel as if I was being watched. I walked along the side of the bridge until I came to a wooded walkway that led to the edge of the bay. The water was oily and dark. The light was getting thinner. I picked up a few pebbles, tossed them in the air, and then threw them into the water. I moved closer to the edge until the water lapped at my feet. What was I looking for, a body to wash up? Yes, this would be the opportune time in those dime-store novels, wouldn't it? I couldn't hope for that. I wasn't even sure he was dead. There was no proof that he existed. No trace, the captain said. But then, where was he? No name, nothing to go on. No trail.

I stared at the horizon as I did that day. I remembered the words he said, things about peace and calmness. I did feel soothed in a certain odd sort of way. I was trying to come to terms with things.

"Why do you do what you do?" he asked me right before he jumped. Why wake up in the morning? You must do something. For me the job was personal. If I had told him, perhaps he wouldn't have jumped.

Just then I saw something floating in the water, drifting with the tide toward me. With each series of waves it grew closer. It was a mask, the mask from the man on the bridge. I'd recognize its ugly countenance anywhere.

I wanted to retrieve it. Sensing that it would slip away from me I waded out to my knees, then my hips, then my midsection. It was as if it were on a string being pulled away just out of my reach. I saw the face, ugly but calm. It appeared to smile at me, then change into another, more personal visage. A last laugh. A last torment. Then I let it slide away with the next wave out of my reach as I slowly waded back to shore.

I never saw the mask again. I went back to the bridge and the bay several times and didn't see it again. The only thing I noticed was the accumulation of dead horseshoe crabs.

I'll never know if I could have talked him down if I told him why I did what I did. The reason was something I never told anyone, even the staff psychiatrist.

My mother drowned herself in our bathtub after taking an overdose of sleeping pills. I was twelve years old. I was the one who found her, floating face up, naked, her eyes open, her head raised halfway above the stillness of the cloudy water. Her face looked just like a mask.

Donald J. Gavron

Background Check

I had been out of work for a little over two years. My unemployment insurance had run its course and unfortunately there was no money left from the government for an extension after providing for tax cuts for the upper 2% of the country. Distribution of wealth? Hardly. Socialism? Maybe for the banks and Wall Street and Chrysler — but not for me.

So, during one of the worst economic depressions since the "Great Depression" of the early part of the twentieth century, I was still out of work, and almost penniless.

Sure, I had some savings, but that would run out soon. I estimate that out of the thousand resumes I sent (mailed, e-mailed, faxed, hand delivered) into the void, I received less than a dozen responses, and half as many interviews.

I'm a graphic designer. I've been in the field for over twenty-seven years. I don't have a pension. I have nothing to fall back on. People who say that unemployed people don't want to work should hand over their jobs to the unemployed and see how they do. Let's switch. On U.I. you only get 60% of your base salary, which in my case cost me $14,000 dollars per year for two years. Who in their right mind would want to lose $28,000 in income?

Of course, a lot of jobs went overseas the last ten years. They're not swimming back to us. I applied for jobs in my field and lesser positions (book stores, retail outlets, etc.), tightening my belt and swallowing my pride. No go.

So, here I was, on the brink of bankruptcy, with no plan. I was tired of thinking out of the box. My relatives had no money. Neither did my friends. I was about to give up. It was January.

Then, a phone call came, an actual phone call about a job.

"I found your resume online," the woman said." I'd like to set up an interview. This is an agency, so we'll have to screen you before we send you on a second interview with our client. Is that all right?"

"Yes."

"I see you have a background in advertising. Have you done any jewelry advertising?"

"Yes. I won an award while I was at the _____ News a few years ago (actually ten). I did ad campaigns for _____ Jewelers and _____ Jewelers and _____ & _____."

"Very good. What computer programs do you know?"

I told her.

"Good. I'll set up an interview. Can you come next week?"

"Yes."

"Tuesday?

"Yes."

"11 a.m.?"

"Fine. I'll be there."

"Bring your portfolio."

"Of course."

"Also two forms of ID, one picture ID."

"All right."

"I'll e-mail you directions. We'll see you next Tuesday. Thank you."

"Thank you. I'm looking forward to it."

Finally, a break. Maybe.

I waited for the e-mail to come. The office wasn't far. I looked over my portfolio and redid some things in it, taking out some old advertisements and campaigns I worked on. I looked for some jewelry ads and placed them prominently in the front of my book. I was ready.

Tuesday came. The weather was cold with a threat of snow or rain; the weather forecasters couldn't make up their minds which.

I wore my suit jacket, paisley tie, dress pants and black Rockports (only because I didn't want to slip on any ice patches}. This was only a preliminary interview anyway.

After several wrong turns, I found the glass encased office. I was about ten minutes early. A young man in a ponytail wearing a white parka noticed me as I went in. I told him I was here for an interview. He knew my name. He asked me to sit down, then got up from the desk and handed me a clipboard with about five sheets of forms on it. It was cold in the office. I tried to make small talk.

"A little brisk in here today?" I asked the guy in the parka.

"The heat is on the fritz. Of all the days, right?"

"Right. Bad day for it."

I plowed through the paperwork. The first sheet was a release form for a criminal background check. The second form was a release form for a financial background check. Why? I don't know. The third form was a consent form for a drug screening. Another form was for a list of references (at least three), and the last was a list of the last five jobs I was at.

This took me about fifteen minutes. I had to give them my social security number. I didn't like to do that but I knew that they would not interview me unless I did so. So, I complied. Steal my identity if you'd like, motherfuckers, I'm tired of it anyway.

After I was done, the assistant asked for my IDs. I gave them to him (my driver's license and my social security card). He went around a corner into a small room and I was concerned for a few seconds that he would not come back.

Hopefully he wouldn't lose one of the pieces of ID in the copier. I think about things like this.

He did return, to my relief, and handed me back my precious documents.

"Did you bring a birth certificate with you?"

"No." My temperature rose half a degree. "Was I supposed to?"

"Sometimes they ask for it. Did she ask you for it?"

"No."

"Okay. Maybe you don't need it. Don't worry about it."

When someone tells me not to worry about something, I immediately tend to worry about it.

I was then summoned to a tiny office, where I sat in front of a huge desk that barely had room for my legs. The chair was uncomfortable. It felt like I was sitting on a plastic milk crate.

The woman interviewer was in her thirties (I presume) and she had a cold. She asked me about my job experience, going over in detail every job I had for the last ten years. She had a salad in a clear plastic container on her desk.

"And what did you do at C_____?"

I told her.

"And what did you do at V_____?

I told her.

"And what did you do at M_____ Corporation?"

I told her. My legs were getting stiff.

Then she asked to see my portfolio. I strained my back leaning over the desk and explained every piece in detail to her.

"I see. I see. I see. Okay. You appear qualified. We're only going to pick about four people to go to the second phase of the interview process. I think you are a good candidate. We'll be in touch."

I shook her hand. It felt cold, like a mortician's. On the way out the assistant with the parka smiled at me and waved.

"Good bye. Good luck," he said.

It was good to make new friends.

I waited anxiously the next few days until I got a call for another interview. Phase Two.

For this interview I reported to the same office. The guy with the parka was gone. A young woman in a business suit told me to go three flights up to a suite marked TESTING. I wore my jeans and a pull over shirt, and sneakers. I figured I didn't need to dress up for this test. But she said TESTING. Did they have something else in mind? Another woman greeted me. She had on a beige skirt and a white blouse. Her hair was black and long and she wore thick, brown-framed eyeglasses.

"Is this where I'll be given my drug test?"

"Yes. Yes," she said, although I could detect a trace of uncertainty in her voice. She was playing with a pencil, poking it into a blank pad on her enormous desk, which someone seemed larger than the other woman had in the previous interview.

I went upstairs. The suite looked like a doctor's office. A nurse in a white lab coat came out and ushered me into a room, where I was told to put on a hospital gown. She handed me three plastic jars on a paper tray.

"In one we would like a urine sample. In one we would like a sample of your sputum. In the third we would like a tiny sperm sample. They are marked for your convenience."

I looked incredulously at the jars, and then looked back at her. URINE. SALIVA. SPERM.

"This is a joke, right?"

"No," she said in earnest seriousness.

"Aren't you going to need a STOOL sample?"

She looked at the chart on a metal clipboard.

"We have you scheduled for a colonoscopy in three days. We will e-mail you the instructions."

"Look, what kind of job is this?"

"You must complete the test if you want to work here. I'm just the messenger."

I went into the room, closed the door, and then took off my clothes. Just then there was a knock. It was the nurse. She opened the door. I scrambled to cover my private parts.

"What the hell?" I blurted out.

"Here is your gun."

"Did you say *gun?*"

"I said *gown.*"

"Oh."

"I have to be in the room with you while we collect the samples. Don't worry, I will have my back turned."

"Oh, that's lovely. Maybe you can help me with the sperm sample when I get to that part of the test?"

She arched an eyebrow, looked down, and then turned away.

I looked at the first jar, labeled URINE. I went over to the toilet and tried to work up some water, but it was no use. I did feel like I was going to shit my pants due to nerves. I was, however, starting to feel a little woody sprouting up, so that may help me with one of the other samples. The nurse's ass was protruding from her lab coat, and there was a patch of flesh visible at the small of her back. She had a tattoo of a rose covered in barbed wire. But it was all too much.

I threw the jars on the floor. She turned around.

"Get out!" I yelled. "Get out!"

She scurried away. I quickly put on my clothes, fumbling with my pants and sneakers. I could hear voices down the hall.

"We must call and tell her," someone said. I opened the door and moved past them like a whisper of wind passing a family of mannequins. They stared at me with dead eyes.

It seemed like forever for the elevator to reach the ground floor. In minutes I was outside, in my car, and driving home down the highway. I was upset, shaking. I decided to stop for a hamburger at a local bar and maybe get a shot and a beer. Or four beers.

I turned into the parking lot. There was a tent erected next to the bar. Before going into the bar I went over to the tent, which piqued my curiosity. Maybe they were giving away free food inside. It was a cold beast of a day though, an odd time for a food tent to be there.

I pulled a plastic drape aside and saw that the tent was filled with tables and dealers, many of them in camouflage gear, with baseball caps that had USA on them.

They were selling weaponry. Automatic weapons, Glocks, rifles, shotguns, Uzis. I just stood there dumbfounded.

One guy spotted me at the edge of the tent and asked me if I was interested in a Glock.

"Me? No."

"This one carries 33 shots. You can do a lot of damage with this." he held it up to my face.

"Whom would I use this against?"

"There've been a lot of home invasions in this area. Gangs are all over the state. Illegal aliens. Refugees. You think the police are going to protect you? They can only react after a crime is permitted, not before. By that time you'll be dead. You're gonna need this once those street gang members get bigger and better organized. A white man doesn't stand a chance these days."

The guy was nuts. I picked up one of the guns out of curiosity. It was light. The dealer, who looked like a football coach, a little like Lombardi actually — big teeth (the front two gapped), thick glasses with black frames, and a crew cut — loaded the clip in. He smiled a gap-toothed grin.

"See how nice that feels?"

I still had a trace of the woody the nurse and her barbed wire rose tattoo gave me while I was in the examining.

"How much?" I asked.

"Three hundred. I'll give you a break. Two seventy-five and I'll throw in three clips, no, four clips of ammo. How about it?"

"What about a background check?"

"Do you have a license?"

I showed him my license.

"You're good to go. American Express, Visa, MasterCard, cash."

I handed him a Discover card. He swept it through a tiny box and printed out a receipt.

"Sign here. Do you need a copy?"

"No." he gave me my credit card back.

"Okay, you're good to go."

"That was easy," I said, palming the gun in my hand.

He looked me square in the eye.

"It's easier than trying to get a job these days. It used to be you walk into a place, you didn't even have to fill out an application. Now they end up putting a microscope up your ass."

"Tell me about it. I just came from an interview."

I told him my story.

"A crying shame," he said. "A crying shame. You see what's happening to this country? I tell you what, I'll give you a shoulder holster free of charge. You seem like a nice guy."

He gave me the holster.

"That's calf skin, real smooth. Oh, yeah, and this here's a permit to carry the weapon concealed. Just print your name on the front and sign it on the back."

"Is this legal?"

"Fuck yeah. We have to protect ourselves, don't we? That's in the Constitution. Life, Liberty and the Pursuit of Happiness."

"Actually that's the Declaration of Independence."

"Whatever."

"There should have been something in there about Right to Employment."

"Don't worry, something will come up for you. Meanwhile the gun will protect you. It will give you confidence, you'll see. We have to look out for each other, brother."

It was funny to me the way he rhymed unintentionally. I shook his hand.

And I walked out of the tent, my gun nestled under my armpit in the holster, hidden in my coat. I had a slight bounce to my step as I entered the bar to have lunch. It was warm inside, but the beer was cold. Ice cold.

Killing Durrell

After school we usually met up in the woods, in a place near the railroad tracks and far from the center of town; it was our usual spot. Sometimes we slipped out early, skipping a last period gym class or study hall.

"Let's go! Let's go! Let's go!" Mac yelled to me.

Mac brought along the booze from his parents' liquor cabinet. They were so wacked they never missed it. They had plenty, and the stock was always being replenished. Mac liked to mix the booze up for us. He fancied himself a bartender, although he didn't know a damn thing about mixing drinks. We'd drink concoctions made with schnapps, brandy, gin and whiskey mixed together. Ugh. It made us shiver, but we drank it. We were in junior high, and we had to invent our kicks. TV and video games just didn't do it for us anymore. There was another world to explore. And we wanted in.

"Just give me the damn bottle, don't mix the fucking thing," Val would say. Reluctantly, Mac would give in.

It was a few days before Halloween. The clocks had been turned back and on this day there was a threat of rain that hung over the school like an ashen curtain. Val and I cut gym and marched across the football field to the woods. A teacher saw us from a distance and yelled something at us. We pretended not to hear him. Val turned around and said, "He's not coming after us." We followed the bike trail down a hill, then cut through a side street of gray suburban houses decorated with cardboard skeletons, witches and sloppily painted pumpkins. The houses looked dead —- dead, but festive. We found some stray chestnuts in the gutter and began tossing them at each other in a mock duel to the death. Each toss got harder, more accurate.

"Cut it, Bryan," Val yelled at me finally, in submission. "Fucking child," he added. I threw a final chestnut at him that hit him square in the back. I was taller and a little heavier than he was, so he didn't want to fight. Not to say that Val was a coward. He would go up to a stranger in the street and kick them in the balls, guys 10 or 20 years older than him, knowing he could outrun them all the time.

We cut through several back yards, hopping fences and dodging someone's mangy dog. After a few blocks the houses disappeared and the woods surrounded us. There was a campground where we liked to do our drinking, and that's where we were headed.

Frankie and Mac were there already, sitting on a picnic table that was partially caved in; a thick board was sticking up in the air, cracked and splintered. The benches were wobbly, and Mac was moving one back and forth with his feet. They were passing a fifth of bourbon between them, the collars of their windbreakers turned up, even though it wasn't that cold out. They gave an old wino some money and scored the hooch from a local liquor mart.

"Then we robbed the drunk," Mac said, laughing and coughing. "Frankie knocked one of his teeth out."

"No shit," I said.

"The old bastard was on his knees looking for his tooth when we left," Mac chuckled, almost in hysterics.

"No shit," Val said.

Frankie pulled a baggie filled with reefer out of his pocket and held it up for us to see. We all voiced our approval. Frankie then proceeded to roll some joints for us to smoke. He was very meticulous and the three of us watched him with anticipation, salivating inside. We passed the bourbon around.

"I hear they kicked you off the team," Mac said to me. "Too bad."

"No loss," I said. The sting of being taken off the football team for repeated infractions and bad grades still hurt, but I wasn't about to show it. Val took a big swig of bourbon and passed the bottle to me. It was down about a third.

"At this rate we'll need a refill soon," Mac said.

"Reefer. Bourbon. All we need are some chicks," Val said. "Frankie, you ready? You're like an artist, man."

"Here you go, perfect dovetail," Frankie said, passing it to Val to light. He struck a match and inhaled swiftly three or four times.

"Sal's bringing some chicks," Mac said, motioning for the joint. My eyes lit up. I was 14, recently on the football team and getting more propositions than I could handle. I always picked the sweetest fruit in the basket, though, the ones I knew I could break in with the sweet talk, then dump on later without the least effort. I stayed away from the girls who gave it up too easily. They were the ones who gave you a hard time later.

"Who's he bringing?" I asked, taking a swig.

"Some new babes. Tara and ..." Mac coughed, not finishing.

"Vicki," Frankie said, not looking up, focusing on rolling another bone. I knew who Vicki was. She had just moved here from Nebraska. I asked Carolyn and she filled me in on all the girls. Carolyn was Frankie's girl, but she was like my pimp, setting me up. I kept hoping she and Frankie would break up so I could bang her. But that would probably ruin several friendships. Maybe I would get lucky with Vicki, though. I hadn't gotten laid in over a week.

We sat around for almost an hour, smoking and drinking and waiting. My ass was getting cold. The bottle was almost gone and the joints were down to nibs. Frankie wanted to wait until replenishment came until he rolled some more. It was still light out, but dusk had a way of coming fast in the woods. Mac and I gathered some sticks and leaves and lit a fire in an old, square, brick grill. We huddled around the fire.

"Fuck, where is he?" Mac asked.

"He'll be here," Frankie said.

"It's getting late. Roll another doob, will you," Val pleaded.

"All right. There's one right here, man. Fuck, there he is," Frankie said, pointing to a clearing in the woods.

"Is it Sal?" Val asked

"Yeah," Mac said.

"Who's with him?" I wanted to know.

"It looks like Phil," Mac said.

"He's got fucking Durrell with him," Val said, disappointed.

"Fuck," Mac said viciously. "I hate that fuck."

Durrell was a kid that we often picked on, but who hung around with us anyway. He was tall and thin and had long brown hair, glasses and a bad case of acne.

"Fucking Durrell," Mac said with resignation. "Where are the girls?"

Val was beside himself. Val once knocked Durrell's tray out of his hands in the lunchroom and Durrell didn't even flinch. Kids would just go up to him and hit him. His glasses were always getting smashed. But we all laughed. He never fought back. He tried to hang with us, to be one of the gang, and the more we abused him the more he stuck around. We even tried ignoring him, but he was still there, like a shadow that followed you and never went away.

We didn't know too much about him. We weren't curious enough to ask. I think his parents were divorced. He lived with an aunt, or his grandmother. He had no siblings. We beat the shit out of him so many times that it became tiring.

Sal, Phil and Durrell came down the path and approached us.

"Where are the girls?" Frankie asked.

"They're coming. Carolyn's bring them. They wouldn't come with us," Sal said with a laugh. That exposed his teeth, which were stained yellow from too many cigarettes.

"Who's got the booze?' Mac asked.

Durrell opened his coat and pulled out a quart of Canadian whiskey.

"Fucking-A," Val said, grabbing it from him. "You just saved your own life."

Val broke the seal, took a swig, then passed it to Frankie.

"What'd you bring this wanker for?" Mac asked, pointing to Durrell.

"He copped the booze," Sal said.

"You guys didn't pay for it?" Mac said, laughing.

"Way to go, Durrell," Frankie said, inhaling deeply from his joint. We passed the bottle around but it never made its way over to Durrell. We were all getting wasted.

"Durrell, go home," Val said, matter-of-factly. We laughed.

"He brought us the booze, let him stay," I said, breaking the ice. Sal finally passed him the joint.

"Give him a drink," Frankie said, snickering.

"Sure," Val said. "But you can't drink out the bottle. I don't want your lips touching this shit. You have to get a cup."

"Where's he getting a cup from?" Phil asked.

"Go home, Durrell. Go home and get a cup," Val intoned.

We all snickered.

Durrell pulled a piece of blank paper out of his pocket and slowly folded it up into a funnel.

"Far out," Phil said. "Give him some, Val."

"Fucking Einstein," Val said. "Fucking Poindexter."

Frankie grabbed the bottle and poured some into Durrell's funnel. He downed it quickly.

"Look at his head snap back. Give him another," Mac said.

Frankie poured, Durrell drank.

"He looks like one of them birds that drink out the cup, you know what I mean?" Sal said, his eyes red, his words slurred.

"No, I don't," Val said. He was getting mad. He didn't appreciate Durrell's ingenuity with the funnel.

Frankie poured another. Durrell drank.

Val stood up and went over to him.

"Fuck, here it comes," Frankie said.

"Durrell, go home," Val said, in dead seriousness. Durrell didn't flinch. I just sat there. We all sat there. We didn't have the energy to move.

"Durrell, go home," Val said again, in the same tone. "Go home, you fucking mutant."

"I forgot where I live," Durrell said, trying to smile, but not knowing if he should or not. His skin was pale with blotches of red. Zits with white heads marked his face like mosquito bites.

As quick as lightning Val slapped Durrell across the side of his face. His glasses went flying, a sight that always provoked laughter. Durrell bent over to pick up his glasses. He wiped them off and put them back on, then sat down further away from us.

"Are you all right?" Val asked. "Did I break a zit or something when I hit you?" Val turned away from him. It was such a common occurrence, Durrell getting slapped, that it didn't faze us. All he had to do was go home, after all. Half his problems came about from hanging with us.

"What happened to football practice, Bryan?" Phil asked. He wasn't up to speed on the story and noticed I was still wearing my football jacket.

"Missed too many practices. Gianelli kicked me off."

"Tough break. Think they'll take you back?"

"Don't know, don't care," I said, taking a big swig.

"They'll ask you back," Frankie said, puffing on a bone. "They need linebackers."

"I heard Morecraft went out for linebacker," Mac said.

"Fuck Morecraft," Phil said.

"Fuck Durrell, too," Val said, coughing. We all laughed. Val just wasn't going to leave Durrell alone. Durrell looked up meekly and smiled quickly, then buried his head between his knees. I couldn't feel sorry for him. It wasn't as if he was real to us. He was an outlet. If anything frustrated us we took it out on Durrell. School. Home life. Girls. Whatever. We took it out on Durrell. He was like our priest.

Carolyn, Tara and Vicki finally showed up. It was getting chilly. They had big burly coats on, scarves and gloves, but no hats. Tara was the only girl with a skirt. The others had jeans. Tara had black fish net stockings and black boots. Their collective visible breath was like a halo of steam surrounding them. The breeze swept up their long manes. Rosy cheeks. Bright smiles. Willing and able. Carolyn brought Vicki over to me and introduced us. Carolyn knew what I wanted. Vicki had long black shiny hair and piercing dark eyes. It wouldn't take me long to get to know her in the biblical sense. Mac had to leave suddenly. He said his stomach was upset.

"You're just afraid of girls," Val said. Mac gave him the finger as he went over the hill.

Tara was the whore of the bunch. I could tell. Val lit her a cigarette and she was talking it up with him and Phil and Sal, deciding who she was going to bang. Carolyn glided over to Frankie and they started to suck some face. We had almost forgotten about Durrell, curled up like a duffel bag near a tree. He was rocking back and forth like he had a ball bearing up his ass. The fire was starting to go out.

"Durrell, get some sticks for this fire," Val yelled. "Make yourself useful, you're not getting laid tonight."

Durrell jumped up and walked past the dwindling flames of the fire. He tripped and almost fell. We all laughed. My eyes teared up. Vicki couldn't keep her hands off me. Sometimes I think he faked falling over to get us to laugh at him.

"Let's go somewhere," she said to me. I knew what she meant and I didn't.

"Where?" I asked, playing cool.

"I'm starving. Let's go to the diner."

"The diner? Shit, I don't have any ... I mean, I didn't think that's what you meant."

"What did you think I meant?"

" ... "

"Hey, I just met you," she said, smiling. "Give me some time to get to know you."

"Time's up," I said, looking at my watch. She slugged me playfully on the arm.

"Beast," she said.

Just then we noticed a commotion in the woods. Sal and Val and Tara were gone. Frankie and Carolyn and Phil turned and ran off in the direction of the commotion.

"What the hell's going on?" I yelled, then followed them with Vicki on my tail.

Down a steep slope was the railroad track that stretched from the abandoned cable works on the outskirts of town south toward the shoreline.

As kids we played on these tracks, setting fires in the woods, hunting for frogs in the ponds that ran parallel to the tracks, putting pennies on the rails for the trains to bend out of shape. At this point in the line there was an old stone bridge that arched over the track from one edge of the woods to another. You could cross the track by descending the steep slope, but then you'd have to climb up the other side, so it made sense to cross the bridge, even though it was narrow and dangerous if you were inebriated. There used to be several stone bridges, but the township was dismantling them every year when they could get the money. We played on this one years ago, walking the narrow strip of stone with no guardrail to grasp. It was about three feet wide and 30 feet long. Durrell was crossing from the other side, a pile of sticks in his arms. Val was pitching rocks at him from a distance. We watched. He hit him once or twice but Durrell made it over all right. Then it started to rain, a light drizzle that became a steady downpour.

"Fuck the sticks, let's get out of here," Frankie said.

"We still have to kill this bottle," Phil said. That was all that needed to be said. Vicki didn't want to drink, but Tara had a few slugs. She had big tits and big thick lips, and she was talking it up with Sal. Soon they went off into the woods to a remote spot. Val finished the last of the bourbon, then threw the bottle at the bridge. He was pissed about something, I could tell. He was almost always pissed. Val started across the bridge, balancing himself by holding his arms out at his sides. Phil followed him across. When they got to the other side, Phil pulled a pint of Southern Comfort out of his army jacket.

"What's the matter? You all chicken?" Val said.

"Free drinks to anyone who makes it across," Phil said. "No takers? Okay. More for us." He took a big swig. Vicki looked at me.

"I'm not going. I don't care what they think," I said.

"That's good," Vicki said, squeezing me tighter. The rain was starting to pick up. You could hear every drop hit every leaf in the forest.

"I'm out of here," Frankie said, but before he and Carolyn could turn to go we spotted Durrell slowly crossing the bridge.

"Fucking Durrell," Val said in resignation. "Come on, you want a drinkie?"

Durrell was trying to balance himself. He was doing all right, then almost slipped. The rain didn't help and his sneakers were so worn out that his toes were sticking through the tips. He made it over.

"Get the fuck back there," Val said. Phil handed Durrell the pint. He took a swig, handed it back to Phil and Val punched him in the stomach. He hunched over and almost threw up. Frankie was laughing. Just then Tara and Sal came back from their rendezvous, straightening their clothes. A few stray leaves were sticking to Tara's stockings.

"What's going on?" Sal asked.

"Durrell," Frankie said, waving his left arm, as if that was all the explanation needed.

"You know, there's a train coming," Tara said.

"Fuck no," Frankie said.

We looked down the tracks to the north. Sure enough, a dim light in the distance advanced, growing brighter. These freights usually ran slow, about 20 to 30 miles an hour at most. Sometimes they were slow enough to hop. This one was going faster, closing ground toward us. We heard the whistle.

"There's a train," Frankie yelled. "Don't cross yet."

"Durrell, get the fuck out of here," Val said.

"Leave him, Val," Phil said.

"Fuck you, Phil. Durrell, get back over that bridge before the train comes. Hurry up, mook. Cross it."

Durrell looked over at the bridge, then at Val.

"If you don't, I'll kick the fucking shit out of you," Val said, clenching his fist. I looked at the train. It was about a quarter-mile away.

"Don't do it, Durrell," Carolyn yelled. Frankie just smiled and shook his head. He didn't care either way.

"Don't listen to her. If you go now you'll miss the train," Val said, trying to sound reasonable.

"Maybe we should stop this," Vicki said. I just raised an eyebrow and did nothing. Durrell turned toward the bridge. Val kicked him gently in the ass.

"Go on. Go on," he yelled.

"Tally-Ho," Durrell blurted out. As he stepped onto the bridge, he slipped and went down on one knee.

"Don't run, you might hurt yourself," Frankie yelled from the other side. Carolyn elbowed him.

"Just stay there, Durrell," she yelled.

"Bryan," Vicki said, looking up at me with concern. All I could think about was fucking her.

"He can either go or stay put, it's his choice," I said to her. She turned away. The rain was splattering us. The woods seemed to take on a thick, wet density.

"They'll listen to you," Vicki said. "Tell them to stop. I'm getting nervous. This isn't funny."

The train whistle blew again, like a banshee wailing. It was getting closer, a dark rumbling theater of inevitability bearing down on the situation. I was about to yell out but the noise of the train surrounded us and drowned everyone out. The ground was shaking. Durrell got up and ambled across the bridge, a step at a time. Val picked up a rock and threw it and missed. The train was almost there. Durrell got to the middle of the bridge and froze; his arms spread like wings. I could see Val jumping up and down, yelling something over the deafening crescendo of the locomotive engine. Then the engine passed under the bridge, a cloud of smoke spreading across our vision, then dissipated just as suddenly as it appeared. The train was slowing. One car passed. Then two. Three. Four. A flat car passed. Two flat cars. Durrell stood there, balancing. Val grabbed the pint bottle from Phil and drank the last of it. He threw the bottle and hit Durrell right in the head, a lucky shot, but the bottle didn't break. It ricocheted onto the grassy slope. Durrell didn't move. There were about five or six cars left. He was trying to hold on. The bridge was shaking. Two cars went by, and then Durrell took a step and slipped. He was pirouetting on one leg now, turning back toward Val and Phil. It was as if everything was happening in slow motion. He flapped his arms frantically, his legs buckling like a ballerina shot by a sniper. He fell off the bridge just before the last car reached it. Vicki hid her head in my chest. Carolyn and Tara were screaming. Durrell dove awkwardly into the corner of the last car. The train bounced him onto the railing where he hit his head and lay there in a mound.

The train passed. I could hear the brakes screeching. The rumbling stopped. Then everything was quiet. There was a focused silence for a few seconds. We were all still.

Then I heard something. A panting, like a wild animal gasping for its last breath. I thought it was one of us. Then I realized that it was Durrell.

Dead Words and More Weird Stories

Uncharted Waters

The ocean rocks with a mellifluous cadence; you are in a cradle of water, the only reality being constant movement and the million pinpricks of an unblemished sun on sunburned flesh. You are rocking in pain, the pain of being alive. You are a survivor, but of what?

Your eyes are closed out of necessity; there is nowhere to hide, but perhaps by force of will you can ignore some of the pain. Your arms are so burned that you feel as if the flesh is hanging off.

How many days at sea now? Two? Three? Three days and two nights. Time. What time? How many hours until the cold night that will chill you to the bone, freezing your marrow? During the night your soul freezes; it becomes brittle, abandoned, a quivering ghost of who you once were. This is too extreme of a contrast to the burning days with almost no cloud cover for relief, baking you like a filet on a grill.

You say your name in order to clear your throat.

"Joseph ... Gallagher."

You say it over and over, a mantra that says that you are alive. Then your throat begins to dry. No water to drink.

Thirst. Ignore it.

Who are you? Thirty-three years old. The same as Christ when he was crucified. Now the sun crucifies you. Who are you? Computer technician. You say it over and over until it makes no sense. Like your name, it makes no sense. Not here. Not now.

Think of the island vacation you took to forget. The small plane crashing with a thud, then sinking without a trace. Two days now. Almost three. Three days, two nights. A solitary raft without food or water. Who knows you are out here? Was there time for a mayday? A May day. A day in May. Who knows? Who cares?

At some point around dusk, when the pain ceases for a short while, you resign yourself to not being found. You let go of the notion of rescue. Something motors by in the water, cutting through the jagged surface. Sharks. Something. Just a twist of the body and you'd be in the water at their mercy, letting the beasts do their job. Over with. Get it over with. But you can't do it. Not this way. It isn't supposed to end this way. Not this way. But you have no control. You cannot take any action to extricate yourself from this situation. You are trapped. If this was school and you were failing, you could study harder. If this was a race you could pick up the pace, push the pain aside and kick higher. If this was the job, you could work later to catch up, come in earlier to give yourself the edge on the prospective calamity of the threatening competition. Sales down. Make more calls. Now, can you dig your fingernails into your flesh any deeper to make yourself feel alive, to keep yourself alive? Will it help? Will anything?

You are resigned to death. You are free for the first time of mortal, material concerns. So be it. Let it go. Let it come down. All fall. All fall down. Ring around the rosie. All fall down.

For years — how many now? — you push the rock up the mountain only to see it tumble down the other side. You walk down and push it up the side of the mountain again. And again. The alarm goes off. You wake up. The same age as Christ. One day you decide not to push. What makes you push? You give up pushing, pursuing.

As soon as you give up, you hear the winding blades of the helicopter, a dark bird blocking the setting sun. A cool breeze blows across your face; water sprays as the raft turns in a twirl. You are in a vortex, spinning. Something is descending. The angel of death? A rope ladder hits the water, slaps across the side of the raft. A tall figure, burly, shrouded, glides toward you as if on wings. Your eyelids hurt, but you raise them. There is an indistinguishable voice speaking to you, distorted by the whirling blades. Someone has a hold of you. Then you close your eyes again, and something on the back of your mind is turned off.

"Where ... am ... I?"

"You're in a Navy hospital. Near a military base not far from the island of Fiji."

"How ... did I get ... here?"

"Rescue helicopter on maneuvers spotted you. Out of the blue. You were on a plane. A plane left one of the local islands at 4:30 p.m., May 6th, four days ago. We got to you just in time."

"The ... lights."

"Your eyes are still sensitive to light; the corneas were damaged, shocked a bit. It'll clear up. Can you tell me your name?"

"Name?"

"I'm Dr. Wilson. Can you tell me your name?"

"I..."

"Nurse, order some..."

"Wait ... it's ... it's..."

"Just relax. Take your time."

"My arms."

"Second degree burns, sun poisoning. Some exposure. Dehydration. You have an I.V. feeding you some nutrients. We have to monitor you for skin cancer eruptions for the next few years, maybe more. You should be fine. It was a close call."

"Years? My head."

"Just a few lacerations. No permanent damage. Nurse?"

"Doctor...?"

"Wilson. Yes?"

"Joseph Gallagher."

"Very good. Rest now, Mr. Gallagher. The nurse will bring you something to help you sleep, to relax you. When you feel up to it you can tell us what that plane was doing near the military base. But, for now, just rest. Nurse. Give him the shot now. Just relax, Mr. Gallagher."

"I don't ... remember."

"You will. You will."

You're back on the raft, drifting in the ocean. It's very quiet. You're not in the hospital. You're wet. The plane has just gone down. There's the wing, sliding into the sea. The pilot, Justin, did not make it out. You've just climbed onto the raft. Where did it come from? Your ears are ringing. There must have been an explosion of some sort. The sun is sinking on the horizon. Rises in the east, sets in the west. There it goes, down in the west. What a beautiful, awe-inspiring sight. Amidst the tragedy of the day he is blessed with a beautiful sunset. It's almost not fair. There must have been some beautiful sunsets in the concentration camps. In the deserts of Iraq. In the deserts of Sudan, Rwanda, the fields of battle in Asia. The sun must have been magnificent going down over Golgotha 2,000 years ago. One man. Help will come. You are optimistic. Help will come. It has only been a short while. You are alive, at least.

Change in tense. Little Joey wakes up in his hospital bed. His parents are by his side. It's Christmas. The nurses have Santa hats on. A wreath is on the door. A tree with flashing lights stands outside the nurses' station. His parents have presents. Long ago. What were they? He couldn't remember. He can't wait to open them except he can't move his arms. His back hurts and he has a headache.

"The doctors all say you'll be fine, Joey. You were lucky," his father says. His father always told him he was lucky when something bad happened. He broke his arm when he fell off his bike delivering newspapers when he was 9 years old. But he was lucky. It could have been worse. He missed the Little League World Series. But he was lucky. He was never able to try out for the team again.

This time he was lucky again. It was just a touch of polio. He'd need therapy. Medications. It was unfortunate, but he was lucky.

"You'll be fine," mother said, echoing his father. She always echoed his father. If he lost his legs and his father said, "Well, at least you have your arms," she would echo him.

Suddenly the hospital room brightened. He closed his eyes. When he opened them it had started to snow, tiny flakes growing bigger, swirling in a rhythm, growing into a maelstrom. His parents sat there. The presents, wrapped neatly in gold and green and purple and blue, sat there on the edge of the bed, just out of reach. He wouldn't be able to reach them anyway. His parents were smiling. They just sat there, frozen, the snow building up around them.

In school he realized that he had to study more and sleep less in order to keep up with the other kids. He had to keep up. So he slept four hours. Three hours. Sometimes he'd stay up for 36 hours in high school. He'd read, study theorems and chemical formulas. All of these things are now forgotten. Pythagoras who?

Joey's hospital room grew brighter. The snow reflected the light and made the light more intense. A bulb in a lamp in the corner of the room burst and the room went black.

Change back. So now you're back in the raft, but only for a moment. It's night and there is a full moon so close you can almost touch it. You can see every star in the night sky. It's cold. You've never felt so cold. Except that time you caught the chill swimming in the lake when you were 10 years old and contracted polio. One star burns brightest in the sky. It has a pulse; it flickers like an electric heartbeat. A light from a million years ago flickers, and then goes out. You wonder what time it is. You wonder what you have done.

"Mr. Gallagher, we have a few tests to do today."

"Sure."

"Can you recall anything about the crash?"

"A little."

"What?"

"There was an explosion."

"Can you tell us why you were out there?"

"No. I don't know."

"The nurse will take some blood from you. Then she'll give you a shot. It will help you relax. It will help you remember. Is that all right with you?"

"Yes. I want to remember. Call me Joey."

"Okay."

The nurse who draws the blood and gives you the shot is a cool blonde, statuesque, ample breasts. She smells like rubbing alcohol and lavender. The serum begins to take effect.

"Maybe later you can give me a massage."

"Sure."

"You can dip your tits in oil and rub them on my back ... my face ... my legs ... my..."

Maybe he says these things, maybe he only imagines he says them. The nurse doesn't react.

She won't be back.

You're in the raft and you're 9 years old. Your arm is in a cast. Three bones broken. You have a pin inserted that will be there the rest of your life. Your mother has packed you a lunch. Peanut butter and jelly. You won't be hungry. You never had it before you went to the hospital. Now it's the only thing you'll eat. You can't get enough of it. You unwrap one of the sandwiches and take a bite. It's a nice day except for the sharks circling. Are sharks fish, you wonder? Yes. Perhaps they are. It is peaceful out on the raft. There is no one to bother you. The last thought in your mind is of someone rescuing you. You don't want to be rescued. You take another bite. It tastes great, chewy. You wish you had some milk. But your mother didn't give you any milk. That was mom, wasn't it? You can't have everything, your father used to say. You stuff the rest of the sandwich in your mouth. You have another one left. You'll save that one for later.

So now you're in the hospital again. Instead of a bed you are lying in a yellow raft, a bright neon yellow raft. You're 1 year old. A valve has gone bad in your heart and you are all alone. Your parents are away on business. Who is taking care of you? One year old. They have to operate. Cut you up.

A tiny incision. Soon it is all over. Your parents aren't around. If they were there they would only tell you how lucky you are. If only you could hear them say it.

"Mr. Gallagher? Joe? Can you hear me?"

"Yes. Of course."

"How do you feel?"

"Okay. I ache all over."

"You've been through quite an experience."

"The serum? Did it work?"

"Yes. We didn't learn what we wanted to learn, but it will do for now."

"I ... ache all over."

"That's life. The human condition."

"I guess."

"You'll be all right in a little while. You can go back to sleep now."

"I need a rest."

"You have all of eternity to rest."

"Am I not asleep now? I feel as if I'm dreaming."

"No. You are awake. You'll be fine. You were lucky. Very lucky."

Donald J. Gavron

The Turkey Just Tastes Different Today

I had to quit my job. Having very little money, I decided to drive my powder blue '63 Chevy Impala from New Jersey to Florida to visit my brother, whom I hadn't seen in five years.

Just as I crossed the border into North Carolina, the radiator started to leak, so I stopped at the first service station I could reach and had a mechanic put a patch on it for me. He recommended I buy a new radiator and that the patch wasn't guaranteed to hold up until I reached Orlando. I told him my situation. He only took $10 for the repair. He was a nice guy.

Sure enough, the radiator started acting up again a few hours later. I had to stop every hour or so and fill it up with water. I drove most of the way with my heater on to keep the engine from getting too hot. The heater helped remove heat from the cooling fluids. My brother told me this.

I drove on slowly, watching the temperature gauge, cursing myself for attempting such an arduous journey. It was October, and I was sweating as if it was July in Dixie. The story of my life was not thinking things through. it was boiling hot in the car. After a while I felt as if I was driving a chariot through the bowels of hell. But I was determined.

Eventually, somewhere in Georgia, I had to pull over and stop. I filled up some old anti-freeze containers and borrowed a bucket from another gas station to fill up the radiator. I let it idle for a while, opened the cap carefully with an old towel, and then poured the water (mixed with some antifreeze) in.

Steam and a smell of burning rubber filled the air. Sure enough, two of the hoses were leaking. I wasn't going to make it. I'd have to abandon the car.

It was getting near dusk. I gathered my knapsack, locked the car, and started to walk down the road, looking over my shoulder from time to time at the steam coming from the dead beast, until I crossed a small bridge and it vanished from my sight. Man, I liked that car. The miles piled up and I hoped to hitch a ride with some trucker before darkness fell.

About a two hours later a 16-wheeler pulled over and I jumped on board. I told the driver my plight but he didn't seem too interested. He had a scruffy beard and looked like he was covered in a light coat of soot. On his head was a baseball cap that said "Free Mustache Rides." Whether he was grateful for the company or not was anyone's guess.

I didn't realize how tired I was. A few minutes later I drifted off into a half-sleep. The truck had to make a few stops to unload some palettes filled with sporting goods. At one point a trooper stopped us. He looked around the cab for a few minutes, giving me the eye, then let us go on our way. Soon we crossed the border and were in Florida.

The driver let me off near a diner in town. It was 2 a.m. and dark as pitch. I bid the driver farewell, never learning his name. He gave me a nod before I exited the cab, jumping out like a skydiver falling from a plane high in the clouds. I went inside and ordered a cheese omelet, toast, and coffee. I took the piece of paper out of my shirt pocket with my brother's address on it and asked the waitress if she knew the location. She did. It was on the other side of town, about 3 miles away.

"Travelin'?" she asked.

"Yeah. From New Jersey. My car died. I'm trying to

reach my brother."

"Some trip, huh?" She poured me some more coffee, then turned and walked away. I was the only customer except for an old guy in a booth at the far end of the diner. He was reading a newspaper and drinking coffee.

Finished with my meal, I ordered another cup of coffee. Then another. The waitress was nowhere to be seen and the diner was quiet as a morgue. I could hear the clock on the wall ticking. Fuck it. I couldn't stay there any longer. It was starting to depress me. Grabbing my bag, I put some money on the counter and set out across town.

Trying to find a house in the darkness on a street where all the houses looked the same is a pain in the ass. After a few false turns, I found the house — #23 Lincoln Road. There was a big tree outside the front of the house, so I sat down on the ground next to it and waited. The coffee seemed to make me tired. I wasn't used to traveling. A mild anxiety came over me and I nodded off. When I woke up, I looked at my watch and it was 5 a.m. Before I knew it, my chin hit my chest and I was asleep again.

I had a dream about my car. My uncle was sitting across from me at an old white kitchen table in his house. He had thick glasses, his hair was slicked back, and he had a white sleeveless t-shirt on. He was holding a stack of money. I handed him $200, and he accepted it like a barker in an auction tent, counting the bills carefully.

"Now whatever you do, don't let that car overheat," he said. Then he leaned forward. "Don't let the car overheat."

"The car has a knock in it," he continued. I want you to take the engine out, take it apart, find out what the problem is, and then put the engine back in the car. But don't forget to put the engine back together before you put it back in the car. Understand?"

In the dream, I was getting nervous, shaking. Suddenly I woke up. It was light out and I felt a chill from the new morning breeze. It was a strange light, like a dimmer switch somewhere was not turned up all the way.

I sat there and stared at the house. It was a drab, one-story ranch. It was pale yellow, with a gray roof and a satellite dish bolted to it (like all the others in the neighborhood). The windows had red shutters.

There was a rock garden in place of a lawn and some tall palm trees on each side of the structure. A rickety screen door guarded the entrance.

My knees creaked as I stood up and I started to walk the narrow concrete path to the house. Five paces, then a step, five paces, then a step, then three wooden steps to the porch. The screen on the door was slightly torn in the upper right corner, and the door was open just a crack.

I didn't know what to expect. I didn't even know if he still lived there. When our mother died ten years ago I remember cleaning out her house. We were carrying a mattress down the stairs. My legs were tired from moving all the furniture that day. The mattress got stuck on the railing. My brother could tell I was frustrated and starting to lose my temper.

"Just take a deep breath," he said. "Take a deep breath." After that I was fine. I always remembered that phrase whenever I felt overwhelmed.

So, I took a deep breath and knocked on his door. The door felt as if it would fall off its hinges. I stood there for a half a minute, and then knocked again. A shudder passed through me. Maybe I was too early, but I was tired of waiting. The house was dark inside. I couldn't see a thing. At that moment I wanted to leave. After all this trouble, I wanted to go.

I knocked again and a form appeared behind the screen. At first it was indistinguishable, like a priest's face in a confessional.

"Yes?" a tiny voice said. It was a woman with short hair.

"I'm Jack Hill. Tim's brother."

"Jack?"

She opened the door and I could see her in the light. She was a tiny, trim woman wearing an olive-colored jogging suit with a designer logo. Her hair was brown and pixie-like. She batted her long fake eyelashes and cracked a wide smile.

"I recognize you from your pictures. I'm Janine. Come

on in, Jack."

She was about forty years old, but looked younger when she smiled. I read somewhere that when you smile the muscles in your face relax. But you can't walk around smiling all the time; people will think you're an idiot.

"Why are you always grinning like an idiot, Jack?" my old art director asked me, right before I told him to go fuck himself and shove his job up his ass.

"Come in, Jack. Come in." She turned around to lead me into the living room. I caught a glimpse of her ass. It was nice and tight, presumably from working out.

"Tim's asleep," she said, whispering, pointing to the couch. "He got in late last night, about three." Shit, I must have just sat down by the tree a few minutes after in walked in the door.

I looked in at him strewn out across the couch, his arm slung across his face, a huge nose and a blonde beard sticking out from under the crook of his elbow. He was breathing rhythmically, and a funny snore was bellowing from his open mouth. He was barefoot, his feet sticking out over the arm rest. Work boots and dirty white socks rested near the end of the couch. He had on an undershirt and navy blue pants.

"Caachooooooooooooooooooooooooorah ... Caachoooooo ... Caachooooooorah ... snort."

"It's nice to meet you," Janine said, guiding me into the kitchen.

"Same here. Glad to finally meet you."

"Yes. We talked on the phone several times. I must say, you are a good-looking young man."

"Thank you," I said, lowering my head. I stared at the kitchen floor. A row of ants was making its way across the linoleum floor from the doorway to the refrigerator.

"You have ants," I said.

"I know," she said in a dismissive tone. "Would you like something to drink? Maybe a sandwich?" She arched one of her pencil thin eyebrows, tilting her head.

"Sure."

"Do you want some coffee; I can put a fresh pot on?"

"No. Just a Coke maybe."

"Sure? It's no trouble," she said, grabbing for the coffee pot.

"No. I had too much already. I was in a diner a few miles away not too long ago."

"Mike's Diner?"

"Yes."

"That's a nice place."

I looked down again at the ants. There was another small group near the sink.

"I'll put on a pot of coffee anyway," she said, turning away again to reveal her tight butt. She grabbed a cold Coke from the fridge and set it down on the table. She was looking inside the refrigerator, leaning into it, lifting one leg slightly off the floor. I think she knew what she was doing.

"Did you drive down?" she asked, still buried in the fridge.

"Yes, up until Georgia, where my car died."

"Oh no," she said, emerging with some cold cuts from behind the door. "I have turkey and cheese. Okay?"

"Sure. Thank you."

"No problem at all, Jack."

She started to make the sandwich, with her back to me, naturally. She had such a round ass and a thin waist and I was getting horny. I imagined what it would be like to mount her from the back. But I had to try and control myself.

I looked at the top of the Coke can and saw a solitary ant near the tab. I flicked it away, not saying anything.

She turned around in what seemed like record time and produced a turkey and Swiss on wheat with mayo, lettuce and tomato, resting on a bright yellow paper plate. Then she put the coffee pot on. It began to gurgle like the death rattle from a small animal.

I took a sip of the soda. It was nice and cold. The kitchen was bright and neat, except for the ants.

She sat down across the table from me, watching me eat. She placed her elbows on the table and propped her head up with her open palms, her fingers gently grasping her cheeks.

I told her the story of my argument with my boss and my subsequent decision to leave.

"I was a studio supervisor in the art department. They made me the offer after I was there for three months because I had a lot of suggestions on how to improve the place."

She stared at me blankly, politely but blankly, nodding her head, the way people stare at you and pretend to hear what you're saying when they couldn't give a shit less.

"It turned out I was just the art director's whipping boy, getting every dirty job. Finally, I had enough. I almost got into a fight with the production manager. Two years. It was the longest I'd kept a job since leaving college."

I took a bite of the sandwich. It tasted odd. The lettuce was soggy, and so was the tomato.

"So, what are you goin' to do now?" she asked, batting her eyelashes, lowering her hands and placing them palm down on the table top. Her hands were small and her nails were short and blood red.

"I don't know," I said, placing the sandwich down and taking another sip of the Coke, which somehow went flat and warm in the space of two minutes. "I thought maybe I'd come down here for a visit. Change of scenery."

"You should have called. Not that I mind."

I could hear my brother snoring from the living room. Janine noticed that I heard him and she smiled, relaxing the muscles in her face.

"I thought maybe Tim could find me some work."

"Tim's out of work," she said, frowning.

"Well, I thought he got in late?"

"Yeah, he was out with some buddies doing some work on a house, picking up some stray carpentry work."

"Oh. Oh. I'm sorry he's out of work." I felt deflated.

"That's okay. He's just laid off for a little while from the plant. They do that every year this time. I get some alimony from my ex-husband. It keeps us afloat. If he mails the fucking check, that is. Sandwich okay?"

"Yes. Fine." It was funny to hear her say "fucking," as if Tinker Bell had suddenly left character.

I took another bite of the sandwich. It was not okay. It

tasted soft. I put it down on the plate. I thought I saw another ant peering at me from the corner of the table. Sure enough, here they came, a small contingent heading right towards me. They stopped by the yellow plate, then climbed onto it like they had tiny ladders and began to carry some crumbs away.

"I'll go see if Tim's awake," Janine said. "After working on that house he went drinking with the guys. He called me. Isn't that nice? Not many guys would be that considerate." She winked at me. As she walked past me I noticed several crushed ants on her left butt cheek.

I looked down at the sandwich again. This time it was covered with so many ants it looked like piece of chocolate cake. Christ, I said under my breath. They're all over the fucking place.

"Do you know you have ants?" I asked, loud enough for her to hear me. She didn't respond. I picked up the plate and threw the sandwich away in a garbage can between the refrigerator and the sink. I dared to look down before I dropped it in, but did not see a single ant in the can.

I looked at the table. The ants were now carrying the crumbs away in tiny wheelbarrows and putting them into zip lock bags.

I walked stealthily into the living room. Janine met me in the hallway. The top to her jogging suit was now unzipped almost to her belly button.

"He's still out for the count," she said, leaning against the doorway. "He might be asleep for a while. Sorry."

"Uh-huh," was all I could muster. I looked inside the living room. I stared at the bottoms of my brother's dirty feet. Janine was staring at me.

"I could wake him up, if you want."

"No. I'll come back later," I said, finally. "I want to walk around for a while." For several long moments I couldn't stop staring at his feet.

"Are you sure?" she asked. I looked up and she was fingering her jogging suit top, running her thin fingers along the jagged silver teeth of the zipper.

"Yes. Yes, I'm sure."

"Okay," she said, slightly disappointed. "Don't forget."

I turned to leave, careful not to step on the ants near the door. I closed the screen door behind me and heard it slap against the door frame like a whip. I looked back through the mesh at Janine's face, now obscured and pixelated by the screen.

"You have ants, you know," I said.

"I know, Jack." I couldn't tell if she was smiling or not through the mesh. "We get that a lot down here."

Walking along the path to the sidewalk, I saw some anthills on the ground in between the rocks in front of the house. I looked at my knapsack, brushing off whatever ants I saw there. They fell off, parachuting safely to the ground.

I turned away from the house and didn't look back. I found a bus depot in town and went up to the ticket window. I had thirty dollars.

"How far will this take me?"

"One-way or round trip?" the ticket taker asked. He was behind a scratched-up glass window with a donut size hole in it. He looked old and tired.

"One-way."

"Not too far?"

"That's okay. Anywhere."

I handed him a bill and he gave me a ticket.

"Leaves in twenty minutes."

I stared down at the newly waxed floor of the waiting room. It was clean, unblemished, and shined so much you could see your reflection in it, almost like a mirror. I sat down in one of the gray plastic chairs, looking around, waiting for the bus. There were no ants or bugs of any kind in sight.

In the corner of the waiting room was a man of indeterminate age in a dirty old coat, crouched in a corner of the floor near a snack machine. He was asleep, his dense black beard smothering half his face. From a distance I could swear I heard my brother snoring.

The Promised Land

I was taking some vacation time off from work. The headaches were getting worse and I went to a doctor to get some medication for depression. I wasn't depressed, but I decided I was at the stage of my life that I needed something. Maybe it would help change me for the better.

"I can give you these pills," the doctor said, producing some sample packets from a drawer.

"Is it a placebo?" I asked.

"No. Of course not. Why would I give you a placebo?"

"All right. Give me the pills. When will I start to see a change?"

"A few days. Closer to a week. It depends."

"What about the headaches?"

"You may have a sinus infection. I'll give you an antibiotic."

"Will it be all right to take the two medications together."

"Sure."

I went home and started taking the pills. A week passed. One day I was watching a show on cable about people searching for houses. A couple from New Orleans was looking at a fantastic house with a fireplace that had a full bath with a shower and hot tub. Christ, what a great place, I thought. The couple didn't like it because it had no room in the back yard for the man's boat. What? They started to irritate me. I turned off the TV.

I started a new routine. In the morning I reluctantly started doing some exercises. Just some low impact stuff. Yoga, isometrics. I took up walking. I bought a tai chi DVD but I couldn't follow the instructor's movements. Once he turned with his body, pivoting his torso, I lost him. I couldn't mirror his movements. Even setting up a mirror to look at the TV didn't help. So much for that. I read some Dickens, then decided to do some writing. No go. I had writer's block. But then again, I wasn't inspired enough to write about anything.

A week went by in a haze. My vacation was almost over. Life was passing me by. I felt like a spectator at a parade. The pills didn't seem to help me, so I decided to go back to the doctor.

"Things are starting to irritate me," I told him.

"How are those pills working out?" He asked.

"Ahhh ... I don't know."

"I'll give you something else. Keep taking the other pills, but take these also."

"What are they for?"

"Anxiety."

"Anxiety?" Now I was on to something. Maybe I was a little anxious. He had no samples to give me. I didn't think I needed the pills but I filled the prescription anyway. The pills cost me $60 for a month's supply. My job did not pay more than minimum wage and the medical benefits sucked. Now I really was getting depressed.

The anxiety medication made me feel more relaxed, but I began to have vivid dreams. In one I was in a house from my childhood. There was no furniture in the house. My late mother and father appeared, but they never said anything. In another dream I was in a barn. My father was lying on a couch that seemed very familiar to me, like it was from an old house we used to live in. He was laying on his stomach in an awkward position and I couldn't see his face.

"Your father's been working hard," my mother said, wringing out an old dishrag to put on the back of my father's head. She had on huge dark glasses and a wig that reminded me of Harpo Marx. But it was my mother. I recognized her voice.

In a few days I went back to the doctor.

"I'm having some strange dreams. I feel like I'm losing my grip with reality," I said to him. I didn't really feel that way, but I thought the doctor might want to hear that I was.

"Strange dreams are common. I'm going to give you another pill. Take this one. Only take the anxiety medication when you feel you need it." I didn't feel like I needed it, but I didn't say anything.

"What's this one for?"

"It's an anti-psychotic. They usually prescribe it for people who have epilepsy."

"Epilepsy? I don't have epilepsy."

"I know. I know. But it can be used for your condition. It's just like giving derivatives of rat poison to people with heart ailments. It'll be all right. If you notice any side effects let me know immediately." He then gave me a list of side effects written on what looked like an ancient scroll.

"That's a lot of side effects."

"You'll be all right. We just have to list them because of the law. But if you start feeling dizzy or you walk into walls, stop taking them and let me know."

"Jesus. Can I drive while I'm taking these."

"I wouldn't recommend it. At least not until you get used to the medications."

I went home and checked my messages. Someone had my resume and wanted to see me about a job. I decided to blow it off, even though I hated my current job. I didn't have the spine to move on. I was too sick, after all, or so my doctor thought. My vacation soon came to an end and I was right back where I was before. No change. I felt the same.

In another month I was taking the anxiety medication every day, in addition to the anti-psychotic medication and the pills for my depression. I felt better, but I was developing some of the symptoms on the scroll. Night sweats, joint pain, vivid dreams, feelings of inadequacy, impotence, beliefs not grounded in reality, lack of connection to my soul, enlargement of my navel, swelling of the ego and a compulsion for baked cookies.

I called the doctor up. He was on vacation, so I went to see his partner, Dr. Parnell.

"Stop taking all of these pills at once," he said sternly. "I don't know why Dr. Graves prescribed them to you in the first place. I want to give you some pain patches and schedule you for an MRI." This was becoming more and more bizarre, and all because I wasn't really feeling that bad about myself in the first place. It was just ennui, but somehow it grew into a big deal.

I went home and took some extra anxiety medication. The pills relaxed me and I drifted off. I fell asleep and had a dream about my brother, who died ten years ago from anaphylactic shock. He was looking directly at me in the dream.

"I want you to start drinking," he said. He was dressed in a doctor's hospital gown, with mask and cap, but I knew it was my brother. He had blonde hair and thin blonde eyebrows. His eyebrows were twitching, like they were signaling me.

"Drinking what?" I asked.

"Start with vodka. That's what I used to drink. Then gin. Then bourbon. Then I want you to start having unprotected sex. With men and with women."

I woke up in a sweat, my arms flailing. The phone was ringing. I let the answering machine pick it up.

"Hello. We have your resume. We are very impressed with your qualifications, especially the fact that you are a drug addict and thinking about becoming an alcoholic. We think you will be a perfect addition to our staff." I erased the message, but at least I was glad I was getting some positive responses.

I called Dr. Parnell back. The girl in the office who answered the phone told me to hold on, then a minute later the doctor picked up. That's unusual. Usually you leave a message and three hours later they get back to you — if at all.

"How are you feeling?"

"I'm perplexed," I said. "I'm worried about my future."

"We have no pill for that. Go see a hypnotherapist, or a tarot card reader."

"Can you recommend someone?"

"No, sorry. I don't know anyone. Call me if anything changes."

"Everything changes," I said.

"True. Talk to you later." Then he hung up.

I looked in the newspaper and found an astrologer. There was a coupon in the paper and I ripped it out. Madame Hilts. She was located in a building on a street in town that I knew. It was a storefront with shaded windows and a glass door with a huge eye painted in the center. I walked there because every time I tried to drive I got the shakes, probably from the pills, or the anxiety I had about driving and taking the pills.

"Come in. Come in. Sit down." Madame Hilts said, opening the door as if she was expecting me. She was a gypsy, about 40 years old and not unattractive, with long dark hair and deep, black eyes. She had on a colorful scarf and wore gold, hoop-shaped earrings. Her cleavage was deliberately showing.

"I have a coupon," I said, and then remembered that I left the coupon home. I forgot to mention that I was beginning to forget things.

"That's only for half a reading. I can give you a full reading for $60 with a 15% discount. We'll round it off to $50."

"Okay," I said. At least it was cheaper than the medication. I stared at her cleavage, then looked away.

"Sit down."

I sat down. She shuffled a deck of cards, made two piles, and asked me to pick one of them. I froze, agonizing over my decision. Sweat was forming on my brow. I just couldn't do it. I got up to leave.

"Where are you going?" Madame Hilts yelled. "If you leave now you'll never know your future. You'll have no future. You'll be ..." I thought she was going to say "dead."

Walking down the street, I thought I heard her calling after me. Maybe she was right. Maybe I had no future. Maybe I was cursed. I decided to take the bus home. Waiting on the corner I thought about the reaction I'd get if I threw myself in front of the bus, the change it would bring to my life. I had no reason to do it, but as time passed, and the longer I waited for the bus, the decision seemed more and more viable to me. But I remembered the gypsy's door as I left. Yes. I thought so. The eye. The damn big eye on the glass door. It winked at me.

Gato

It wasn't just a howl, it was a vicious guttural scream, almost like a human scream, as if someone or something was being attacked and its soul was being torn from its body. The nasty screeching was terribly disturbing. At first I thought it was some animal caught in a trap, or more likely on a fern bush, outside and near the window of my parlor. It started, then stopped, and then started up again, each time worse than before. It was slightly after 1:00 a.m.

I have nothing against cats, my wife and I owning two ourselves. They are very precious to my heart, and at times I believe they keep me from going insane. But this cat, this night, was disturbing not only me, but causing my other two cats to become frantic, running up and down the stairs, stopping dead in their tracks whenever the screaming occurred, their ears poised and pointed at the ceiling, their necks stretched to new lengths. Jumping up from my chair, I turned the television off.

I picked up Bubbles, my ginger-colored tabby. His heart was pounding and he was exhaling through his nostrils. He struggled with me and didn't want to be held. My little white cat, Mousey, would not come by me. She ran over by the fireplace near the window where the monster lurked outside. She then jumped on the couch, looked around, looked at me (I was standing now, a flashlight in my hand, ready for anything), then settled down on the top of the couch, her tail wagging furiously, as if caught in a storm.

Shining the flashlight through an opening in the blinds I could see nothing but tiny patches of moonlit ground behind a maze of bushes in the corner, where another unit faced my condo at a right angle. Then I saw it, a dark gray furry monster probably about fifteen pounds, with a silver collar around its neck. Then I saw the light from a flashlight coming around the corner. It was my neighbor, as I suspected, and it was his cat, and he had come outside to retrieve it. I moved away from the blinds and turned my flashlight out. My neighbor was talking to it, trying to coax it to him.

Now there is a rule against leaving pets unattended in our condominium complex. It's in the by-laws. I told my neighbor about it on more than one occasion.

"Aren't you afraid your cat might get hit by a car?"

"No," he said languidly, "my cats have always been good that way."

I called the property manager and told him I had seen the cat out may times; I identified the neighbor, and said I had spoken to him about it.

"I'll send out an e-mail and a letter to everyone, just so he thinks he's not being singled out."

One Sunday morning I was walking with my wife, getting some weekend exercise, when I saw my neighbor sitting on his porch smoking a cigarette. Not five feet away from him was his cat, walking around, about ten feet from the road.

"I see you're still letting your cat out," I said, calmly.

"Hey, listen. It's my cat and I can do what I want."

My wife grabbed me by the arm and tried to lead me away.

"Yeah, that's right — the rules don't apply to you, motherfucker. We don't let our cats outside. Go fuck yourself."

"What are you trying to start trouble for?" My wife tugged at my arm.

"I'm not. I'm not. It's him."

I have hypertension, and my wife saw my face getting red.

"Let's go home," she said. "I don't want any trouble."

"I'll be all right. I'll be all right."

We walked around the block, talking about what to do, then walked in silence back to our home.

Not long after this incident we found a dead bird near our bird feeder (having a bird feeder was not against the by-laws) and my wife found a tiny dead rabbit near a bush by the pathway in front of our door. It was the neighbor's cat, I thought. It had to be. My rage grew inside me. Don't do anything, I said. Don't do anything, you'll wind up in jail.

Then came that dreaded night. After he wrangled his cat inside, I sat down, took a tranquilizer, turned on the television, and then fell asleep in my chair about a half hour later.

My anxiety about the cat was growing. What was I going to do? No one seemed to care, especially the owner. I could kill him (my neighbor), but then who would care for my wife and my cats? No, that was not an option. I could catch the cat and take him away somewhere, but I'd need some tools: a pair of thick gloves so it wouldn't scratch me, a cage of some sort, and some cat food to use as bait. This was an enterprise that required focus and concentration, as I would have to watch for the cat and perhaps lay in wait for several hours. My wife was usually a sound sleeper. She went to bed listening to a radio talk show from Boston every night on her headphones, so she wouldn't be an issue. I would be as stealthy as a cat. Yes, a cat.

The tell-tale sign that the cat was out usually happened when my neighbor left his garage door open. I could see the light on the ground in the courtyard from my bedroom window. That would be the signal.

First I went to a local gun-and-game store to pick out my trap. The owner helped me choose a Duke 1110 1-Door Trap, 32x10x12 in size. It was impressive, and looked like an oversized basket that young boys used on their bicycles when they delivered newspapers back in the day. It cost $34.00 without tax. The best bet would be to place it under my front deck, in the corner nearest the spot where the animal was howling that night. It was easy to set, and I put a small amount of cat food in a tiny dish inside. Then I waited.

It wasn't long (two or three days?) after the trap was placed that my prey was caught. I heard a metal rattle, then a series of growls, then more rattling. It was all happening under the deck. Time was a factor. The creature in the cage (if it was the cat) had to be gathered away and into my car before my brain-dead neighbor had a chance to tune in to the howling, and before my wife knew what I was doing.

Grabbing my keys, I slipped into my boat shoes (my shirt and shorts were already on) and calmly and deliberately locked the door behind me, tiptoeing toward the corner of the deck. There it was, as dark as night, in the cage, a silver collar around its neck. The coat of the creature sparkled in the moonlight, and its bright green eyes shone like twin traffic lights signaling *GO.*

Grabbing for the handle of the cage the beast swiped at me and grazed my hand but did not draw blood. It began to scream in a stuttering wave as I fast walked to my car. The streetlight was out, but the moon illuminated my actions like a searching cycloptic eye. This had to be quick. Unlocking the door, I threw the cage into the back seat and started the car, patiently letting it warm up. No one could see inside (I removed the bulb from the overhead light), or so I thought. It was late, well after 3:00 a.m. in the morning, and there was no sign of anyone wandering around my suburban neighborhood. A sudden burst of adrenaline swept over me. At last I would be rid of the tormenting beast, the foul creature that haunted and upset my beloved cats, my wife, and me. And it would be a favorable alternative to knifing my neighbor in the back and dumping him behind one of the warehouses in the industrial center.

There was enough room to swing my car around to the corner of my street, facing the intersection. I waited until there was no sign of traffic and then I drove across the intersection and toward the group of condos across the way. In my rear view mirror I thought I saw a flashlight in the brush near my unit — perhaps my neighbor investigating the noise — or maybe I had imagined it. My heart raced as I thought, *What if it was him? I would be suspected in the disappearance of his bloody cat!* There was no turning back now. He could prove nothing, and after I was done there would be no evidence to support his allegations, if he presented any.

Driving through the back roads of the condo units I came to the highway that would lead me north to a desolate locale I had scouted days before. I would deposit the beast there. It was quiet, except when I hit a bump and a muffled growl came from the cage. I could feel its rage.

"Now you're going to get yours, you miserable animal," I said out loud, full of triumph. As I drove, the moon was directly in front of me, watching me.

It was an hour later and I began to yawn. I needed a coffee, but didn't want to stop anywhere until I got farther away, or until I got rid of the damned thing.

Turning off the highway, I drove along a back road to my destination. The animal began to whimper, perhaps sensing what was to occur.

"Shut up, you cursed thing."

I had a bottle of water in the front seat and I flipped the top off and threw the contents over my shoulder in the direction of the animal.

It cried out as if was just seared by acid.

"Shut up, you crud."

As I continued, the animal settled down, but the moon, the accusatory, watchful moon, was directly in my line of sight.

A thousand curses ran through my mind as I realized the gas gauge light was on. I was in the middle of a secluded area surrounded by woods. There was a station I remembered passing along the way, but instead of turning back I looked for a spot to pull over off the road and unload the animal. Was I far enough away? Forty-three miles according to my odometer. The car began to stutter, then stall. I couldn't be out of gas, I just couldn't. The gauge light had just gone on. But, yes, I was forced to pull over. What to do? What to do?

I couldn't leave the cat in the car for fear of a police car arriving on the scene. The only thing to do was unload the foul animal, dispose of the cage, and then walk to the station.

The moon was hidden behind the trees now. It was no longer there to witness the dirty deed. But the glow was still omnipresent in my mind. This time I procured a glove from the trunk (in addition to a flashlight) and reached into the back seat for the handle. The creature growled.

"Go on, you filthy little pisser, go on and try it."

It did lunge for my hand, but I felt nothing. Swinging around, carrying the cage, I turned my flashlight on and saw a clearing thirty paces ahead. Intending to just let the cat out, the lack of proper distance from our origin point concerned me. I had heard tales (no pun intended) of cats finding their way back from many miles away. This cat also had a tag on its collar, which looked like a phone number. Obviously, the creature was known for wandering off and being lost. I had to dispose of not only the creature, but also the tag identifying it. There was no way to safely reach into the cage and grab the creature and remove the collar. I hadn't thought of this. There was no *Plan B*. Instead I found a tree and began to slam the cage against it, hoping to knock the animal unconscious, then dump it out, take off the collar, and finish the pest off with a rock — if I had the nerve. Half a dozen slams against the trunk did no good, except to make the mangy thing more cross. Setting the cage down, I looked for a rock, and found one about a foot and a half in length and of ample girth, enough to do the job. Was I up to it? I could see that the cat was dazed, so I opened the gate and waited for it to emerge, my flashlight in one hand and the rock in the other.

It staggered out and moved in a backward *S* towards me. Closer. Closer. Then I rammed the rock at the beast with a fury I did not think myself capable of. The rock glanced off the cat and the cursed thing let out a scream and ran into the woods.

Surely it will die of the wound, I told myself. If it was wounded. I tossed the cage far into the darkness, hoping that the noise would drive the animal farther into the wooded abyss.

My heart was pounding as I ran to the car. I dropped the glove somewhere on my way, but I didn't bother to look for it. Who in hell would be looking for evidence — a glove, a cage, a dead cat? I was being paranoid.

Taking the keys and locking the car I made my way down the road, waving my flashlight, hoping to catch a ride. I looked at my watch. It was 4:10 a.m.

I walked until my legs ached. Holding the light, I saw something emerge from the woods on the right side of the road. It scared me enough to send a shiver through my body and make me rigid. At first I thought it was the cat, but it was only a possum. It turned to look at me, the animal's eyes aglow from my flashlight.

"Scat," I said. "Scat."

My heart beat faster. I could feel the vein in my neck pulsating. I began to jog, slowly.

The dark expanse of woods appeared to be talking as the wind blew, sending a cacophony of sound to assault my senses. I wondered about that beast of a cat. Where was it? Did it surge further into the woods, or did it turn back toward the road? Was it following me? I suddenly felt a million eyes staring at me.

I arrived at a gas station, sweating profusely, the eye of the moon still intently watching me. I looked around and imagined the green eyes of the cat glistening from the shadows. The warm lights of the station bathed everything under its canopy in a surreal white glow. Everything was blanched and drained of shadow.

A lone station attendant was in the office watching a movie on a 13" TV and eating a microwave burrito.

"I ran out of gas," I said, and then chuckled. He looked at me quizzically.

"I have a gas can in the garage. Pump yourself some and you can pay me when you get back."

"Do you think I can get a ride to the car, it's a couple miles up the road."

"I can't leave the station, man. In fact, you're lucky I'm still here. Just can't stand facing the old lady tonight. Know what I mean."

"Yes, yes, I know precisely what you mean." I was a little too understanding.

"New kid, our third. Stays up all night, wailing like a banshee. Waaaaaah. Waaaaaah."

I just stood there, a shit-eating grin on my face, listening.

"All right. All right. Let me close up. You fill the can, I'll drive you up the road. You're going north?"

"Yes."

"It gets real dark up there. Dangerous. A lot of curves, not many lights. You hit a ditch they may not find you for a few days. Okay. Let's go."

I filled up the red container. The gasoline smell consumed my tiny personal atmosphere. It felt intoxicating. Some gas spilled and washed over one of my cuts, burning the wound. It was like a jolt.

Turning my head, I saw his truck backing out of the garage, the annoying back-up horn shredding the silence. When I looked back to the container, I saw, standing on the other side of the pump, the miserable beast I had just dumped in the woods.

"Mother of Jesus," I said, almost falling on my ass. I fumbled with the cap and closed the container.

"Scat. Scat," I yelled. The beast let out a hiss and bared its teeth at me. "Go away. Go away." It just stood there, mocking me. *Try to get rid of me, will ya?* it seemed to ask.

"Let's go," the attendant said, his tow truck idling like a bull in a rodeo pen. I jumped in, watchful not to let the cat follow or attack my heels.

The next ten minutes were the most worrisome and frightening minutes of my life. The attendant waited on the side of the road as I poured the gas into my car. All the while I was looking down the road for the monster, wondering when it would arrive. It never showed up. I started the car.

The attendant waved and he turned the tow truck around and I followed him back to the station.

It was waiting for me, I surmised. It would let me get back, let me lapse into a false sense of security, then attack and get its revenge. Why Why Why had I done this stupid thing? It was too late to be conciliatory. I had to kill the animal at any cost, and chance gave me the opportunity to do so.

As the attendant was putting his truck away, and as I was filling up my car, I poured some more gas into the red container, then placed it in my back seat, covering it with an old coat. Hopefully, the attendant would be too busy to notice. If not, I was prepared. It astonished me how the adrenaline and tension of the night's events had caused my concentration to focus so acutely.

"I'm locking up for the night," the attendant said, having already closed the garage doors and shut off the lights. The only lights that remained were some dim fluorescents overhead, just enough to illuminate the lot.

"What do I owe you?"

He looked at the meter on the pump. "Twenty-five bucks." As I was counting the money he suddenly remembered the missing can.

"Where's the gas can?"

"Oh shit," I said, feigning ignorance. "I must have left it in the field. Christ, I'm sorry. Can I pay you for it?"

"No. I have some extras. It's not like there's some sentimental attachment to it or anything. I'll snoop around for it tomorrow."

"I appreciate it. I appreciate all your help."

"No worries, brother. Stay well."

"I'll certainly try."

And I was off, headed home. But I had one last plan to implement. The monster was sure to follow me, as it followed me to the gas station.

I began to emerge from the dense woods. Streetlights appeared, a traffic signal. More signs of civilization followed. A strip mall with an all-night convenience store; a liquor store, a nail salon and a pizza parlor — all closed. Another closed gas station, and then a cemetery.

The cemetery gates were open and I drove slowly along the narrow road. I parked on a hill. The back of the car facing the entrance. The streetlight gave some illumination. The houses nearby were all dark and silent.

If the beast came it would come up the path (or so I hoped). I poured most of the container on the asphalt road, spreading it out back and forth. Grabbing a flare from the trunk, I waited.

No, it wouldn't work. There was too much risk. The monster was too smart. I threw the can away and got back in the car. *Fuck it.* I would think of something else.

I backed out slowly, just clearing the gates. I heard the car scrape the road, and hoped my tailpipe survived. It was almost 6:00 a.m. Dawn would be breaking soon. All my efforts were ruined. Hopefully my wife was not awake to interrogate me on my foolish night's adventure.

Half asleep, with the purple and orange rays of dawn breaking, I crossed the intersection near my house. THERE WAS THE CAT! Right in my way in the center of the intersection. I stepped on the gas and felt it crunch under my wheels. A minivan coming from my right slammed into me and I shot up onto the curb and took out a light pole. I was dazed. The morning light was seeping through. Early morning traffic was stopped. I felt warm blood flowing down my brow. A chorus of voices rang out.

"I didn't see him. I didn't see him."

"Is he all right?"

"Stay there, fella."

"Call 9-1-1."

"I did already."

"There's a cat in the road."

"Is it dead?"

"I think so. I think he tried to avoid hitting it."

He couldn't be more wrong. The beast. I had to verify that it was the beast that had tortured me all night, and all those nights before.

"You should stay still, mister."

"The ambulance us coming. The police will be here

soon."

I wouldn't bet on it. My car was totaled. The front end was smashed. Steam from the radiator was rising with a foul metallic stench. All that mattered was the beast, the monster, and the tormentor of my soul. Was it dead?

A small coterie was gathered around it. There it was, lifeless, its body crushed, its silver collar wrapped around its neck. I moved closer and reached over to look at the silver tag. It had my neighbor's address and phone number on it. I turned it over, and before I passed out I started to cry, after reading the name written on the tag:

Blackie.

Nails

I was walking to the library around noon one day, bright August sun overhead, a trace of warm wind, temperature in the high 80s, when I saw a nail in the gutter. I thought it over for a moment, and then decided to bend down and pick up the nail, which I then threw on the grass. When I was stooped over I noticed some more. There was also a bolt, rusted and decayed, and some tiny screws. What the hell, I'll pick them up and toss them also, I told myself. Maybe I would prevent someone from getting a flat tire. It would be good karma to prevent someone from being greeted by a flat in the morning as they were driving to work, having picked up a tiny screw from the gutter. Or perhaps someone would be going out in an emergency, to the hospital, something. I thought about that Ray Bradbury story where the guys go back in time and one of them steps off the path, kills a butterfly, and changes the course of history. I was altering the course of the world. I'd be a hero, or at least an existential one. The self-help tapes I'd been listening to said: "Do good. Feel Good. Good will come to you." We'll see.

After disposing of the objects, I continued on my way to pick up the books and films I had on reserve at the library.

It was a twenty-minute walk, and my doctor had been getting on me to exercise more because my cholesterol was too high. My left leg strained a little as I stepped, from my gluteus maximus to my hammy to my shin. The chiropractor said it was a muscle pull, and that it would go away. It's been three weeks.

A few minutes later I spied some more nails. What was going on here? Was there some messy construction crew that forgot to clean up? I walked along for a minute and saw a trail of bolts, screws and nails leading around the bend near the condominiums along the curve of the road.

I stood in the shade of a small tree and thought about this. I'd started something, I decided, so I had better finish it. I picked up a plastic bag near a tree across the street and started to collect the refuse. How many cars was I saving from repair? How many people was I unknowingly making happy? It took me over an hour. I tried to count, as I was fetching them from the gutter, but lost count somewhere around three hundred and forty-seven. Rust had scraped off on my fingers and I was sweating, but I wiped my brow with my forearm because I didn't want the flakes of rust to get on my face. What an ordeal I had tasked myself into doing. It was like a nightmare except for one thing: the pain in my leg was gone.

I approached the library and was maybe a hundred feet away from a garbage can when the bag broke, spilling the contents onto the courtyard near the entrance. I just stood there like an idiot. A few people walked by, women with their kids, an old man with a cane. The sun grew hotter on my neck. Expelling a great sigh, I looked down and saw in the pile of nails, screws and bolts what looked like some words spelled out.

YOU ARE DOING GOOD WORK
BUT YOUR LIFE WILL NOT BE BETTER FOR IT

I stared at this message for what seemed like a half hour, but what must have been only a minute. My vision telescoped in, then faded back on the letters. Okay. Maybe.

Maybe the message was right. I scooped up the pile of nails and bolts and metal bits and pieces, put them in the bag, then placed them in a garbage bin near the front door. I then went inside and got a drink of lukewarm water from the fountain near the restrooms.

Sitting in a chair near the magazine racks I leafed through one of the books I had picked up from the reserve desk. It was "Infinite Jest," by David Foster Wallace, the writer who had committed suicide several years ago. I read a little, and then almost fell asleep, thinking of purpose, of existence, that everything we do is for nothing unless we attach a meaning to it, because in the end it is all meaningless but unprofaned.

I walked home with a bounce in my step and unlocked my door with a slight tremor. A moment of epiphany came over me. I felt possessed, purposeful. I gathered up some trash bags and a scooper left over from when my dog passed away. I went up and down the streets of my neighborhood picking up nails, screws, bolts, bottles, ketchup packets, plastic bags, beer cans, milk cartons, used condoms, candy wrappers. I found some change, even a five-dollar bill. I dropped them off at the Quick Check in the jar for kids with cancer. Then I went back to gathering together and disposing of anything I could find that soiled and spoiled the neighborhood that surrounded my life, my quiet, happy, self-contained life.

Inactive Shooter

Ben usually visited his local library in Port Lansing two or three times a week. He reserved films, CDs and books on his computer at home. Before that he spent close to a fortune buying these things from stores online. Now he was out of work and forced to sell most of his CD collection to supplement his U.I. to stay afloat. He was forced by necessity to find out that the wonders of the library brought some much needed, harmless and distracting entertainment to his life.

Nothing seemed to be going right for him recently. He worked for over 25 years in the advertising field. During that period he worked at a local newspaper for ten years. The last advertising agency he worked at suddenly closed due to the economy, and he was out of a job. He collected U.I., but the money he received wasn't enough. He continued to look for work; his search came up empty. He sent out resumes, made phone calls, networking with friends and acquaintances to land something, anything. This only produced disappointment. He even applied to the local Drug Mart chain as a photo tech to process film, but never got a call back. He even followed up twice. One week he went in to pick up a free 8x10. It was a special offer he received by e-mail, and he noticed a young kid working the counter. He thought he would never find a job.

He talked to his friend Tom on the phone once a week. Tom had a job in Delaware, but was struggling also.

"People I know that are working are stressed out and the people I know that are out of work are stressed out. It's a different type of stress, but it's still stress," Tom lamented. "You work and work and work yourself to death like a slave on a galley ship. But when you're out of work, like I've been many times, you stress out about money, making the mortgage. You can't even go to the movies."

"That's why I go to the library, Tom. I had a library card when I first moved here, but only rarely used it. They have everything. You just have to wait three or four months until the new movies come out and you can see them for free. I can't tell you how much money I saved by not spending money on a ticket to see a lousy film."

"You have to find a way. I know I learned to get along without a lot of things."

The subject changed to other things: baseball, football, films, and the future. After an hour, the conversation exhausted, they returned to their lives.

Ben got to know the people who worked behind the desk who checked the items out. One girl, Alicia, advised him on an ointment to help with his eczema. They were friendly, except for one or two. The women were generally glad to see him, and after a while he knew their names. The indifferent ones seemed to be the men.

"How are you doing today?" Ben asked one of the clerks, a mild-mannered fellow with a white beard.

"I'm here," he said, not looking him in the eye.

Another time, after a particularly heavy snowfall, he asked one of the fellows, a tall, bald gent with glasses, how he liked the snow.

"Thanks for asking," he said dismissively.

They had a way of doing things he didn't like. A fat, unkempt little guy held onto his keys while he checked for reserves. Why? All he had to do was scan his library tag and give Ben back his keys; but no, he had to put them off to the side. Several times Ben reached over the counter to retrieve his keys.

Another guy, in his mid-forties, didn't check in Ben's returns right away. He put them off to the side. Ben liked to have the items checked in. So when he went back home and checked his computer, he could see the items returned. He was paranoid about having something lost and being blamed for it.

"Can you check those in, please? I'll wait."

"Oh, I'll check them in, don't worry, sir." The desk clerk's name was Tim.

"Can you do it now? I'll wait. I just don't want to see anything lost in the sauce," Ben said.

"Lost in the sauce? I never heard of that one," he said with a wry smile as he scanned the items and took them off Ben's list on the computer.

"It's an old saying. Not too old though," Ben said. He tried to be nice to everyone. Some self-help guru said that you should try to make at least three people smile during the day. Tim wasn't smiling though. People are strange, Ben thought.

After a few years some of the desk clerks left, transferred to other branches, or just retired.

One clerk whom he took a liking to was Liza, a married woman with two high school daughters. She was about ten years younger than Ben, who was fifty-two. They talked briefly about films or books. They never seemed to like the same things. Oh, that was awful, Liza said. I thought it was good, Ben replied. But they would just laugh and share some brief moments of levity. Tim took a liking to her. She was married. He was married. And so, he thought never the twain would meet.

Several places in town were regular stops for Ben. He ate at the sub shop twice a week. On Wednesdays there was a pizza slice special at Paul's. He patronized the coffee shop almost every day, and, of course, the library. Ben's wife Tina worked, and was their sole support. The pressure to get a job was not too high until his U.I. ran out. Weeks passed, then months, then a year.

"When are you going to find something?" Tina started asking more and more.

"I'm over fifty. In advertising that's old. It's not like I have some special skill."

"Try and go to school. Take a class. Do something."

"And start over from the bottom? At my age? Besides, I have time to write my novel. It's coming along pretty well."

"The chances of getting published are astronomical. You're better off buying a lottery ticket than sending out those stories. They probably don't even read them. Everybody thinks they're a writer."

"Well, that's encouraging," he said, being sarcastic.

"Well, you better find something quick. I don't care where. Get something at the fast food place."

"I'd rather cut my throat."

"Let's hope it doesn't come to that."

And so it went. Coffee, sub, library, pizza, week after week after week. He downgraded his satellite to save a few dollars a month, but now he couldn't watch the Mets games. Hell, they would only lose anyway. He scrounged around for more CDs to sell. He looked at all the books he had that he would never read. Ben started to donate some of them to the library.

The library had a small section near the entrance, not far from the check-out desk, that sold used paperbacks and hardcovers (and occasionally some DVDs and CDs). It was on the honor system. A patron found a book and placed the money in a metal box on a thick rectangular pole near the section. The change often made a loud noise as it slid down the throat of the box. Sometimes, if Liza was on, she'd yell out "Hey, keep the noise down there." Ben smiled. He liked her.

One day Ben was in a particularly bad mood. Something was off. People seemed distant. The weather was gloomy, overcast. Liza was working the desk when he came in to pick up some films.

"I saw this one, it was pretty good."

"I haven't seen it yet."

"You'll probably hate it," she said, smiling. It was a light moment in a rather gray day.

Ben went over to the used book section and perused the racks. There was a tall guy with a wool hat and heavy coat staring at the books on one of the tall racks against the wall. It was a narrow room with bins for the pocket paperbacks; and racks for the hardcovers and trade paperbacks. Ben looked at all the shelves and bins and went over to the spot where the tall man was standing. The man appeared to be reading a book he was holding, but he was standing there, blocking Ben's way. it was obvious the man knew Ben was there, he just didn't feel like moving.

"Excuse me," Ben aid, reaching for a book on a shelf right in front of the man's face.

"Yeah, well that's human nature, I guess," he said. His face was pock marked and he had a scruffy salt-and-pepper beard. He looked to be around Ben's age, but who could tell?

"You're just standing there reading a book," Ben said softly. "Can't you just move over to the side a little?"

The man didn't say anything, and he didn't move.

"You're a fucking jerk," Ben said under his breath as he turned to leave, just loud enough for the man to hear him. The jerk said nothing; he just kept looking at his book. Ben left in a huff. My entire day is ruined, he said to himself. He wanted to go back and punch the guy, or wait for him outside and confront him. But no, his wife knew his temper and always tried to dissuade him from confronting people. A long time ago he got into trouble. He knew the consequences.

He stopped for a coffee, and then drove home. His wife was out shopping, and Ben sat down, drank his coffee, and watched TV. There was a movie on that he'd seen a dozen times. He watched it again.

An hour later he turned on the local news channel and couldn't believe what he was seeing and hearing.

"There are reports of an active shooter at the Port Lansing Library Branch. Two people are dead and several wounded. The man is on the loose and police are combing the area. Local schools are on lockdown. The shooter was described as a tall man in a burly coat with a wool hat and heavy beard." Then they put up a photo.

It was the guy, the guy he had the run-in with in the used book section. Christ Almighty. Two people were killed. Oh, God, don't let it be...

He watched the news for the rest of the day. His wife came home with a car full of groceries.

"What are you doing, I have bags to bring in."

"There was a shooting at the library."

"What?"

"The library. My library. Some ... maniac."

"Jesus Christ, is it safe anywhere in this goddamn country? Too many guns and too many psychos with access to them. It was a man, of course?"

"Yeah."

"Sure, always trying to extend their penises."

"I was there today."

"What? When?"

"About four or five hours ago. It happened about an hour after I got home. I've been watching the news ever since."

"Jesus Christ. Let's get these groceries in. We'll find out more later. Take your mind off that."

"They said two people were killed. He's still on the loose."

"I have ice cream and chicken that needs to be put away. I'll do it myself."

"No, I'll help." He got up and helped his wife put away the groceries.

Ben was numb, but nervous. He took a tranquilizer and sat back down, watching the news. What if he set the guy off? What if it was his fault? You're a fucking jerk, Ben said to him. Maybe that was the straw that set him off. Did he have a gun with him when he called him a jerk? Did the man go home and come back? Was he looking for Ben, or did he just want to kill some people? He remembered now that Liza said they were giving all the employees active shooter drills because of what was going on in the country. All the school shootings scared people, especially since the children in Newtown were butchered by that disturbed kid whose mother bought him a gun. Anything can happen at any time to anyone. It was the way of the world. More guns were bought, but did that make people safer? Congress didn't even want to mandate checks on people. Suppose this guy had a history of mental illness? Ben always thought that anyone could snap at any time. There was no profile for an active shooter. And a lot of times it just stigmatized the mentally ill. He felt helpless.

At eleven o'clock at night they announced that they had apprehended the man, Tyler Brock, 47, of Bannertown. They didn't mention if he purchased the gun legally, but they did say he was being treated by a psychiatrist. After first notifying their families, the names of the two people who killed were revealed.

June Yang and Liza Peeples were the victims.

It was his friend, Liza. Ben was paralyzed. God, was it what I said that set him off? He couldn't tell his wife. He was too embarrassed. He couldn't sleep. He changed the channel. "The Wizard of Oz" was on and he watched it as if under hypnosis.

"We're not in Kansas," he kept repeating. "We're not in Kansas."

He woke up the next day and watched his wife get ready for work. She put on her clothes, brushed her teeth, and combed her hair. He was looking at her, observing every detail. He noticed things he never did before. She was alive. He was alive. He took a deep breath. But the daylight appearing through the bedroom curtain was different.

"Is something wrong?"

"Huh, no," he said, sitting on the edge of the bed.

"What do you want for supper?"

"That's twelve hours from now. I don't know."

"Well, think about it. The recycling goes out today. Put some birdseed out by the trees. Try and take a walk. It looks like a nice day." Everything she said had a hint of irony.

"Okay, bye." Then she was out the door. After a few minutes he regretted not saying he loved her before she left for work. Suppose I never see her again, he thought. Suppose she gets into a car accident, or has a stroke, or something else. God, he said, I shouldn't be thinking these things.

He combed the papers for the next few days and saw the obituary for Liza. The paper listed the funeral parlor holding the viewing, the church, and the cemetery. He knew where they were. For some reason he couldn't bring himself to go, to see the other people. Maybe he'd visit the cemetery. Maybe. He didn't go back to the library. The things on his reserve list lapsed. They would go back on the shelf, or back to the other libraries they came from. It didn't matter. He lost his interest.

He called his friend Tom and talked to him about what happened.

"You can't blame yourself. This guy was a psycho. He was going to do this anyway. People are fucked up in this country. He had a lifetime of shit building up, most likely he never even remembered what you said."

"Maybe he came back thinking I'd be there, that he'd find me and kill me."

"You're talking nonsense. Look at what happened to that football player last week. His car got rear ended on the highway by a Humvee. He got out of the car and the guy shot him. He had a wife and three kids. The nicest guy in the world everyone said. The football player, I mean. The guy who shot him had a record, was treated for psychological problems. But he could get a gun. Just another day in America. look at the guy who shot up Fort Hood. A fucking Army base. And the guy was a psychiatrist. It happens all the time."

"But it shouldn't be. We shouldn't accept these things."

"Listen, Ben. The world was a fucked-up place before we were born and it's going to be fucked up long after we're dead and buried. Look at the history of the world. Chaos. Barbarism. Torture. Murder. Starvation. The Holocaust. Just try to live your own life and move on."

"How can I?"

"Have you found any leads yet on a job?"

"No."

"Well, I got to get back to work. Deadlines. Busy season."

"Yeah. I know the feeling. Deadlines. I'll see you later, Tom. Good talking to you."

"We'll talk again soon. There are some concerts coming up. We'll get together. Keep your mind clear."

"All right."

"All right. Just take it easy. Don't beat yourself up."

"See you, Tom."

The Bug Man

"My plants are under attack from insects," I said to the bug man, standing behind his desk.

"Aren't they allowed to live also?" he shot back at me, never looking up from the ledger that was laid open on the top of his desk.

"Huh? What?"

"I asked you: 'Aren't they allowed to live also?'"

"Sure. What? They're pests."

"So are you."

"Beg pardon? What the hell are you in business for? You've got a truck and all these cylinders filled with bug killer — what are they for?" I drove all the way down to his office after work, and all I got was grief. I was frustrated into taking action by the invasion of insects on my domicile, and now I was getting more frustrated by the bug man's attitude. Two other bug men I stopped at were closed. I was desperate.

He looked up and me, the thick lenses of his eyeglasses distorting his blue eyes. He grinned.

"You're right," he said. "Sometimes I forget myself. Sometimes I think it would be better to exterminate the entire human race."

I calmed down a little. I was desperate for help.

"Maybe you're right," I said. I played along.

"Don't you think the Hindus were onto something when they said they we all come back as insects, elephants, cows and other creatures. Aren't we all God's creatures?"

"I don't know. Maybe. All I know is that the bugs are tearing up my place. Maybe their karma is off."

"Maybe they need a place to stay."

"Look, are you playing games with me?"

"What for? Are you?"

"Aren't you going to help me?" I tugged at my collar and loosened my tie. It had been a long day.

"You didn't answer my question," the bug man said. I looked at his fingers as he pawed his ledger. They were tinted green at the tips, and his nails were yellowed with deep vertical cracks in them.

"What question?"

"The Hindus. Weren't they onto something? The reincarnation thing?"

"I don't know. I don't know. Perhaps."

"Perhaps, he says. I mean, one of those bugs could be a relative of yours, or relatives."

"What?"

"We go through stages in life," the bug man said, wiping his nose with a dirty rag.

"Yeah. Stages. Well, if they were relatives of mine — if they were relatives of yours, wouldn't you want to help them get to the next level? Wouldn't you want to put them out of their misery here in this existence and get them to the next level?"

"How do you know they're miserable?"

"What is this being filmed for a fucking reality show?" I was getting flustered. My blood pressure was rising.

"No. This isn't a reality show. Well, maybe you're right. I never thought about it that way. Maybe we should help them get to the next level. But, who are we to judge?"

"Are you insane? What are you in business for?"

"Pest control."

"Don't you have any clients?"

"I do."

"Well, why can't you help me instead of bickering with me? What's the problem?"

"Because I can tell that the bugs are not the problem in your life. I think you are the problem."

I looked up at the ceiling. There was an old rusted ceiling fan wobbling counter clockwise and squeaking.

"Don't you know a lot of these bugs help eat other bugs. Spiders are very good at getting rid of pests."

"Maybe I should contact a fucking spider."

"Maybe."

"I've wasted enough time here."

"Have you? I think you have more time to waste."

"You won't help me?" I asked, trying one more time to get through to him. The next bug man was thirty miles away.

"Sorry," he said, looking down at his ledger again. "I can't help you."

"Sure. Sure. I bet you are. I bet you're sorry. I'll just go somewhere else."

"What makes you so sure they'll help you?" he asked, looking at his ledger and slowly turning the pages with his green fingers. "They might be Hindus."

"They'll help me," I said with defiance. "They'll help me."

"Don't be so sure," he said.

I turned away and opened the door to the shop. A tiny bell sounded as I exited. I thought I heard him snickering as I walked to my car. Thirty miles. Would the next bug man help me?

California Replicant, Inc.

"Two guys walk into a bar," Jeff said as he slithered onto the stool next to me at the Pine Room. He waited a beat, then said, "Ouch. Get it — Ouch." I got it. No formal greeting, just a kind of frat joke to break the ice where there was no ice to break.

"Hi, Jeff, how are you?" I decided to take the formal route. We shook hands the normal way, without styling.

"It's been a while," he said, motioning for the bartender and fondling his smart phone. "What is it — a year?"

"Maybe, maybe. I lost track."

"Been so busy, you know?" He was talking to me, looking around the bar and stealing glimpses at his phone, his attention never in one place for very long. "No rest for the weary."

"You can say that."

"I just did." We laughed. The bartender came over, white shirt, black vest, red tie, his face like a frozen oracle. I ordered an imported beer and Jeff ordered a domestic and a shot of tequila, the expensive kind.

"So, what's the occasion, Ron?" He asked the question, looked at his phone, then clicked a button before putting it back in the pocket of his Brooks Brothers suit. Jeff looked fit and artificially tanned. He kept his blonde hair short, almost military style. The man exuded confidence.

"I'm still out of work. Just collected my 99th check a few weeks ago. Now I'm living on savings."

"No prospects?"

"No." I shook my head slightly and slowly. "Resumes, applications online. You can't walk into a place anymore. You have to apply online."

"Temp agencies?"

"Nada. Nothing."

The drinks came. Jeff slipped the bartender a twenty.

"On me, old friend."

"Thanks, Jeff," I said.

"Don't worry about it. I wish I could help you a little financially old buddy, but ..."

"I'm not asking for that. I have some savings left from that inheritance. I'll be all right for a while."

"Cheers. To better times." We clinked bottles. Jeff downed his shot, and then his phone rang, a weird ringtone that sounded like a spaceship taking off. He wiped his chin, took the phone out of his pocket, looked at the message, shook his head, and then placed the phone back in his pocket.

"Idiots," he said in reference to the call. "Anyway, yeah, I know how it is. I was out of work for a while. It seems that everyone I know is either out of work or working and pulling their hair out. If we could bottle stress in this country we'd have the fucking Chinese beat, goddamn it."

I fondled my bottle, balancing it on the bar.

"It's tough," I said. "No doubt. You either have money or you have no money. Anyway, I don't mean to sound like a whining bitch. That's not why I called."

"You're finally coming out of the closet?" Jeff snickered, then motioned for the bartender, his right finger making a circular motion down at our drinks.

"No, nothing so cliché. I must tell you something you may not — I mean — that might seem strange, odd in fact. Maybe unbelievable."

"I'm intrigued." The bartender came over, pointed to the drinks. Jeff nodded and the bartender was off to fetch some refills.

"I've been having these dreams. It started about a month ago. I woke up early, around six a.m., did a few things around the apartment, and then started to feel tired. I lay down on the couch for what I thought would be a few minutes, but I fell into a deep sleep. I had a dream I was in a future world decimated by war. There were two people I did not know, standing near some demolished buildings in a city somewhere. I think it was Los Angeles. I was wearing a type of suit made of illuminated blocks, sort of like Legos. I had a helmet on, like a bike helmet, also with these little illuminated blocks. I was kind of a super hero. Or cyborg or something, I don't know. But I felt that these people depended on me for something."

"I've never been good at dream interpretation. I don't go in for that Freudian nonsense."

"Listen. There's more."

He looked at me askance, raising his bottle to his lips. It was the kind of look that said, "Is this why you asked to meet me?" I'd known Jeff a long time, maybe twenty-five years. We were close for a long time, then drifted apart. I got married and divorced. He went to jail for three months for insider trading. The refills came.

"Two more shots, two beers, and some nachos, with chili. Jeff, anything for you?" He laughed. Fucking comedian. He knew I was trying to be serious so he was being deliberately funny. I knew he didn't want to hear what I had to say but I was going to say it even so.

"The dreams. There were more. Let me start over. I had this first dream about a month ago. I didn't think anything of it. A week after that I had several more. I was in the same location with different people. One time I was in a church. There was a little girl playing the pipe organ in front of the congregation. When she finished her solo, everyone cheered and she came running down the center aisle of the crowded church toward me. I grabbed her and hugged her and everyone cheered. It was as if we had been reunited after a long time. Then, here's the strange part. On her dress was a blue ribbon, and it said 'California Replicant, Inc.'"

"Did you recognize this little girl?"

"No."

"You never had any children, did you?"

"No." I was lying. My little girl died when she was three.

"Have you read that Nabokov novel? Maybe it's got something to do with that."

"I'm serious, Jeff."

"I know. I'm just trying to relieve the tension."

"Look Look Look. I am deadly serious. There were other dreams. I was fighting for my life. I was in this suit, this illuminated suit."

"Seriously, Ron. This sounds like the film *Tron*. Maybe you saw the film and dreamt it. Shit happens like that."

"I did see the film years ago."

"There was a sequel. Just recently."

"I know. It sucked."

"Except for Olivia Wilde." His smile quickly faded when I looked him in the eyes. He grew serious, as only he could.

"Look, Ron. I've never been good with things like this. I don't try to analyze my life. I just try to survive. I have a nine to five, it's a ball buster, but it's a job. I make six figures, not as much as when I was a trader, but it pays the rent. I tell you what. I can loan you some money. See a doctor. An analyst."

"I appreciate it, Jeff. I don't need another analyst. You sit in a room with someone telling and tell them your problems and all of a sudden it's six years later and you still have the same problems. No. I need an objective mind. I need someone like you who has absolutely no experience with these things. I need a fresh perspective."

"I don't know what to say."

The bartender carried a steaming plate of nachos over to us and set it down on the bar. We just looked at it.

"Tell me some more," Jeff said, downing another shot.

"It was so real. It was as real as if I am talking to you. You know when you have a dream and then you wake up and you remember it and you know it was a dream. This is as if I left here and the outside world was demolished and I had that suit on and I was waiting to fight some malevolent evil that was trying to take over the world."

"Don't take this the wrong way, Ron, but this sounds like a Philip Dick story. You've heard of him, right?"

"Sure. *Blade Runner*. Ridley Scott film."

"I read a lot of science fiction in school. Hell, I didn't have to study much with my dad in business all those years. Anyway, this sounds like some dream like in *The Matrix* or something. A simulacrum."

"I've thought about all of that. It's not a simulated reality. It's not an alternate universe. Maybe something or someone is shooting me into the future as a warning to tell the people of our time to get their shit together or an apocalypse will come down on us."

"You sound pretty certain."

"I know. I can feel it in my bones."

"I mean, how can you be sure? How do we know what is real? I mean. This sounds like a sci-fi script, or *The X-Files* or some shit like that. From what I can tell from your story it sounds reminiscent of a lot of films, maybe *The Terminator*, or some old *Outer Limits* episodes. Not to trivialize what you're saying, but you watch this stuff, then it seeps into your dreams. Maybe they're hallucinations, or flashbacks from all that acid you took in college."

"I never said they were hallucinations. And I didn't experiment with drugs that much."

"You never know. All it takes is one bad acid trip."

"Maybe I'm dead and I don't know it."

"Sorry, Bruce Willis, that script's been filmed already."

I was starting to get annoyed. But maybe Jeff was right. Could I be this divorced from reality?

Jeff picked at the nachos. "Fuckers are hot," he said, licking his fingers.

"I'm sorry, man. I suppose this is the moment where you reveal yourself to be this government agent and you're onto me because I've discovered this crack in the simulacrum and I'm seeing the future." I laughed and exhaled.

"And the government doesn't want anyone to know the apocalypse is coming because they're prepared for it and don't want the little people to survive."

"Yeah, and McConnell's behind it all. He's the cyborg."

"You're not far off, buddy." Jeff raised his beer and took some swigs. I noticed, just above where his watch was a tiny logo that looked almost like a radiation logo they put on x-ray rooms or in power plants.

"Where did you get that tattoo?"

"What? Oh, I've had that for a while. It's to let the handlers know I'm a cyborg so they won't accidentally put me in a relocation camp." He kept a straight face for a second or two, and then laughed.

"You have a better imagination than I do," I said, my voice shaking, laughing uneasily. Maybe he wasn't joking. Was Jeff that good an actor?

"An old girlfriend had one. It's a fraternity."

"I never saw a fraternity tattoo."

"I'm going to get it taken off when I get the time."

He wasn't going to elaborate on the tattoo. We ate the nachos and had two more beers. The bar was starting to get crowded.

"You ever watch that show with the alternate realities?"

"The one on cable?" I asked.

"Yeah. They have like three realities. I used to like the show but it got too complicated. Anytime a writer has boxed himself into a corner he comes up with some wrinkle like time travel or an escape into an alternate universe to solve his problems."

"I wish I could escape. Maybe I'm the cyborg."

"Maybe you are. In your dreams. Look inside your shirt. Maybe you have the human race on a wire, like that

Ellison story. Christ, you better hope Ellison doesn't get wind of this and sue you. He's very litigious. You need a job, my friend, something to keep you busy. Freud said work is important to mental health."

"I thought you didn't believe in Freud?"

"I'm just trying to cover all the angles. I said I don't believe in him, I didn't say I never read him. Look, let's keep in touch. I'll scope out my place and see if there's a job there for a trainee or something." He wrote down his number and put it on the bar.

"I appreciate it."

"I have to go. The grind, the grind. Man, when you get back to work you won't have time to think, much less sleep or dream. I'll see what I can do."

Jeff got up. We shook hands. He took the check, and then left another twenty on the bar.

"Have a few on me. With what this joint charges you might get a bottle and a half out of that."

"Thanks, Jeff. Thanks a mill."

"No worries, buddy. Stay well. Call me." He made that silly motion where the thumb and pinky are stuck out and held up, pointing at the ear, as if people really held a phone that way.

Cyborgs. Reality. Simulacrum. Alternate universes. Time travel. I wish I did believe in all that nonsense. Was I insane? How could I know if I was or not? The bartender came over and reached out and pointed at the plate of half-eaten nachos.

"All done?"

I looked at his hand. There was the same tiny mark on his wrist that Jeff had. Or was I imagining it?

"Yes. I'm done," I said, trying not to let him notice that I noticed. Maybe I was wrong. I was never more confused in my life. Jeff certainly didn't help much. Maybe I'd take him up on that job offer. Maybe I was thinking too much. Maybe the next dream would leave a bigger clue. Dreams. Illusions. Dreams within dreams. Poe wrote something about that.

The Happy Man

Part I

Bentley Soames had a problem for many years, ever since his father died. He did not know how to enjoy himself. No matter what he did or where he went, there was no joy in his endeavors.

Sex was an ordeal. Movies seemed so phony and trite. Books held no value for him. Food tasted the same. The news on television, and television in general, was boring. In speaking with other people, which he rarely did, they all seemed to agree that TV was a cultural wasteland.

Music was an indifferent affair. Classical music was too dense and boring. Modern music tended to be facile. Nothing held his interest because he didn't enjoy anything. He didn't know what to do. Because he had inherited some money, enough to keep him comfortable for the rest of his life, Soames had a great deal of uneventful situations to look forward to. Suicide was not an option because it seemed too dramatic a statement, and he didn't like drama.

One day he came upon an idea as he was sitting at home staring at the wall. He would place an ad in the paper. It took him a full day to compose it and when he finally brought it to the local paper to place in their classified section it read:

**PERSON WANTED FOR CONFIDENTIAL WORK
MUST BE HAPPY AND AVAILABLE FOR 24 HR
PERSONAL SITUATION TO BE EXPLAINED
555-187-4949**

The ad cost him $25 for the week. In a few days he started getting calls and set about screening people.

Soames got calls from prostitutes, massage parlors, professional clowns, and some calls with just heavy breathing on the other end. Finally, he hit upon a likely candidate and called him up on the phone.

"Hello. I am returning your call about the position."

"I'm sorry. Which one? I've been … "

"Of course. Personal situation. Confidential. Happy man."

"Oh, yes. I'm a little perplexed about that ad, but I've been out of work for so long I thought I'd give it a try."

"What is your name?"

"Dryden. Peter Dryden."

"My name is Bentley Soames, Mr. Dryden. Do you consider yourself a happy man?"

"Happy? I guess. Relatively speaking."

"Can you tell me a little about yourself? Make it as personal as you like."

"Okay. Let's see. I was born in New Hampshire. I went to college in Rhode Island. Didn't graduate. I've held a number of jobs …"

"How old are you?"

"Ahhh … thirty-two."

"Fine. Sorry for interrupting. Continue, please."

"I've never been married."

"Are you gay?"

"No. I'm not gay. I've had some long-term relationships. Say, what is this all about?"

"Basically, I'd like to know if you are a happy man, if you enjoy your life."

"Seriously? Well, sure. I guess so. Why not? It beats the alternative," Dryden said, laughing.

"Do you laugh often?"

"Only to keep from crying."

"I see. Very good. Let's set up a meeting. Do you know Cavino's Bistro on South Street?"

"Yes."

"How about 5:00 p.m. tomorrow?"

"As long as you're buying."

"Of course."

"Wait. Just one thing. You aren't in some sort of ... cult, are you?"

"No. Why do you ask?"

"It all just seems strange to me."

"You will show up tomorrow?"

"Yes. I need the money."

"I'll explain it all to you then."

Soames hung up the phone. For a second he almost formed a reflexive wisp of a smile on his face, but it was just an itch from a shaving cut that occurred earlier that morning.

The next day Dryden entered the restaurant about 5:05. The maître d' told him that Soames was in a corner booth and was expecting him. It was dark inside, so dark that it made Dryden think that there must be something wrong with the electricity.

As Dryden approached Soames he came into view as the veil of darkness gradually lifted. Soames was a man of medium build with no distinguishable features. He appeared to be about 65 or 70 years old and he had on a three-piece suit, as if he was going to a funeral. He was drinking what looked to be a Mojito.

Dryden had on slacks, an old pair of black Reeboks and a gray jacket with brown patches on the elbows. He also wore an open-necked chartreuse dress shirt.

"Mr. Soames?"

"Sit down please, Mr. Dryden."

Soames made no effort to get up or to shake Dryden's hand. His face was expressionless, like a mannequin.

"Order a drink and something to eat," Soames said.

The waiter came over and took their order. Dryden ordered a California burger medium well, with sweet potato fries, and a bourbon and coke. The waiter looked at Soames, who crooked his neck and ordered in a manner that suggested that this was his usual meal ordered out.

"I'll have a tossed green salad with no dressing and a steak, rare, and a pot of black coffee which I'll take right now."

The waiter nodded, then dipped back into the shadows.

"Do you eat here often?" Dryden asked.

"More often than not," Soames said dryly. "Let's get to the point. I am the victim of an emotional quandary that I have tried to analyze to no avail. There is no Freudian or Jungian reason for it, it just is. I can't enjoy myself, in a subjective sense. I've given up trying to explain it because it only adds to my misery. In a sense, I am looking for someone to be happy for me."

Dryden looked at Soames as if he was studying a sarcophagus in a museum.

"You're kidding, right?"

"No. That's the dilemma."

"I don't understand."

"Don't try. I'll pay you two hundred dollars a day plus expenses, but you will be at my beck and call. If I phone you will have to meet me. Do you have a reliable car?"

"Yes. What do you mean, meet you? I told you I am not gay." He whispered the last word.

Just then Dryden's drink and Soames's coffee arrived.

"I'm not talking about that," Soames said, his face still expressionless. Dryden sat back in his seat and raised his drink to his lips.

"You'd make a good poker player, you know, mister?"

"I don't enjoy the game. Or any games for that matter?"

Dryden gulped his drink halfway down, then crunched on some ice cubes. Soames poured himself some coffee just as his salad arrived.

"Why don't you just get a hooker, smoke some grass, and go to the circus or something?"

"Please. Everything that could be tried has been tried. Don't try to analyze me or figure me out. This is the situation. It is what it is, so to speak. Are you interested or not?"

"Sure. For two hundred a day plus expenses I'm very interested."

Soames went into more detail. Dryden listened, seemingly hypnotized by the events unfolding. Their dinners arrived. Dryden ate, ordered two more drinks and a slice of cheesecake and a small pot of coffee as Soames talked, deliberately slicing his steak and chewing it as if it had no taste. Everything about Soames seemed odd, even the way he ate. Even what he ate. It was mechanical, as if he had all the time in the world and he was in no hurry. Dryden finished eating, but Soames was only half way through his steak, having avoided the salad to that point.

"That's all, Mr. Dryden. Can I call you Pete? It's just more efficient for me that way."

"Sure. What's your name, by the way?"

"You must call me Mr. Soames. For what I'm paying you I believe I deserve that courtesy."

"Fine," Dryden said, wiping his mouth with the cloth napkin and sliding out of the booth.

Soames stared at his steak, slicing a piece of gristle away. He didn't look up at Dryden.

"I'll call you at noon tomorrow," he said, slicing off another piece of steak like a surgeon.

"Thanks for the meal."

Then, Soames looked up.

"Did you enjoy it?"

"Yes. Very much. Thank you."

"Good. Very good. Now we're getting somewhere. Here's a retainer. Two hundred dollars." Soames put his knife and fork down. He opened a leather wallet and plucked out four fifty-dollar bills and placed them on the table near Dryden.

"Spend it wisely. Good-bye, Pete."

Dryden left the restaurant and fumbled in his coat pocket for a pack of cigarettes.

"What have I gotten myself into?" He said to himself.

Part II

The call came precisely at noon. Dryden woke up with a hangover. After leaving Soames he went to a sleazy bar and drank himself silly. He woke up at 7:00 a.m., threw up, and took some aspirin. He thought yesterday was a bad dream. Then the phone rang.

"Hello?"

"Pete? I want you to meet me at the corner of Brick and McMillan at noon. Can you manage that?"

"Yes, sir."

"Dress a little more upscale than yesterday. Add a tie and some black leather shoes, if possible. Shine the shoes please. No smoking. I can smell it a mile away."

"Whatever you say, Mr. Soames."

The phone clicked. Dryden thought for a second about blowing the whole thing off, but there was something about Soames that piqued his curiosity, so he decided to see it through for the time being. If this gig lasted long enough he would be able to move out of this dump over the dry cleaners, get a car, and maybe do something with his life.

Dryden got a cab to the corner where Soames was to meet him. Sure enough, there he was, standing like a statue, dressed in the same suit, or another suit of the same design, but with a different tie, blue with thin white stripes. He got out of the cab and approached his benefactor.

"Good morning," Dryden said.

Soames turned and faced Dryden.

"It's 12:16, Pete. Get a grip on yourself." Soames stared at him like an X-ray machine.

"You were drunk last night?"

"Yes. A little. What's it to you?"

"Let's get this straight or we can end this here with no harm done. You will not do anything of a pleasurable nature without my consent. If I am not there to give consent you do not do anything. You don't watch TV, you don't drink, and you don't fornicate. Understood?"

"Can I take a piss? Sometimes I get a rush taking a bowel movement. Is that okay?"

Soames braced himself.

"I see your point. All right. We'll make some stipulations. But the things I just mentioned you are forbidden to do. In addition to reading material of any kind except traffic signs. I will tell you what to do."

"Jesus, this is getting weird."

"And no going to any places of worship either."

"You're a strange man, Mr. Soames."

"This is a controlled experiment. Let us proceed."

During the afternoon Soames brought Dryden to an ice cream parlor, a sub shop, took him to see a comedy at the Rialto (buying him popcorn and nachos), and then to a Turkish bath on Mendelssohn Avenue. While they were in the Turkish bath they talked, wrapped in towels, sitting on a bench, with the steam rising from some hot rocks that some of the other patrons occasionally poured water onto with a ladle.

"What kind of afternoon did you have? Describe it to me."

"It was fine. This is all right."

"What I want to know is: did you enjoy it?"

"Yes. It was strange, but all right."

"Describe it please. I don't want to pull teeth here."

"The ice cream tasted good."

"Why? Details. Details."

Some of the other people in the bath were starting to stare at Soames and Dryden, and eventually they began to leave.

"I want you to think. Think. What was it about the ice cream that made you feel ... joy?"

"I haven't had ice cream in a while. It was cold. And sweet. It brought back memories of when I was a child."

"Yes. Yes. Yes. That's what I'm getting at. The connection. The *why* of the matter. What specifically makes it enjoyable, Pete? Understand?" All the while Soames was taking notes in a black ledger.

For a second Dryden felt a connection with Soames. The sinister veneer dropped for just an instant to reveal a pitiful creature, incapable of enjoyment, or of love, who wanted desperately to be happy. Dryden knew what he was after, and he began to open up more.

Yes. It reminded him of what it was like to be a child again, going to the movies with his parents, eating a sub sandwich on a Saturday afternoon following the movie. It didn't really matter if the movie was good or bad, as long as it took you away from the grim reality of school, work, and the daily grind. It reminded him what it was like before his parents were killed and he was put into the care of relatives who didn't want him.

The Turkish bath was relaxing, like having your soul massaged. He never really considered it before, but with happiness the air tasted sweeter, people looked kinder, animals made the heart flutter. Women turned you inside out. He told Soames this, who marked it all in his ledger.

In the weeks to come Soames took Dryden on a tour of the city and beyond. They ate fine meals, smoked expensive cigars, went to Atlantic City and Las Vegas (where they had a setback when Dryden lost some money and did not seem happy). They read books together. "The Sun Also Rises," "The Adventures of Huckleberry Finn," and "Ulysses." Dryden thought the Joyce novel was "kind of dense." They saw films. Antonioni. Hitchcock. Kubrick. Welles. Soames built a movie room with HDTV and they screened almost every new and old film. There were hiccups along the way, to be sure. A man bumped into Dryden on the street and didn't apologize. Dryden took exception and shoved the man, who started a fight. The police came and they whisked Dryden away. Soames bailed him out and got the charges dismissed. When he got out of jail Soames asked him about the experience.

"It was exhilarating, I must admit," Dryden said.

"Excellent. Excellent. Details. Details, my boy."

They toured Europe, touched on Asia, and drove down Route 66 in a '63 Chevrolet Corvette convertible. Dryden really enjoyed that trip, except for the flat tire in Phoenix.

Soames bought him women, but the experiences left Dryden empty, even though they were enjoyable.

Through it all Soames was a master at handling situations. Money greased a lot of gears and Dryden was glad to be part of the machine.

"Are you happy, Pete?" Soames always asked. If Dryden said "No," then the question was: "What's missing?"

Invariably Dryden couldn't put his finger on it.

"The nature of happiness is fleeting," Soames said time and again. "Life is made up of moments. Some good. Some bad. I see that now."

Finally, after several months of intense living, they sat down in an expensive restaurant in New York and had a talk, a summit meeting as it were, of events up until that point.

Soames ordered his usual meal, and Dryden, trying to impress him, ordered the same.

"We have to get down to the idea of enjoyment and happiness," Soames said, chewing on his salad like a rabbit. He chewed, sipped some coffee, wiped his mouth, and then continued. "What is it that you enjoy and what is it that makes you happy?"

"That's the question then, isn't it?"

"I must know."

"Why is it important?"

"Don't be impertinent, my boy."

"You want me to be happy. I've had some enjoyable experiences that have undoubtedly enriched my life, but overall, am I happy? I can't say that."

"Then this experiment is a failure. If you feel no joy, then I feel no joy."

"I've felt joy, but not happiness."

"We're chasing our tails here. We have to up the ante."

"How? How do we do that?"

"What one thing above all else would make you happy?"

"Knowing I didn't have to die," Dryden said dryly.

"Don't be a nit. That's why people theoretically enjoy life — because of its brevity."

"Theoretically," Dryden said with resignation.

"Well, do we let this go or not?" Soames posed, already half out of his chair, his meal unfinished.

"One more thing," Dryden said, stopping Soames in his tracks. "Love."

"Love?" Soames sat back down.

"Yes. Romance. Carnal love. Not just desire."

"Yes. I see it. We must find someone for you to fall in love with."

"It just doesn't happen that way. You just don't find someone."

"We'll contact agencies, matchmakers, we'll hang out in bars. That's what people do." Soames gestured for the waitress, an attractive blonde with blushing red lips.

"My good woman, will you look at this man, please?"

She turned her head and looked at Dryden.

"Is this someone you could fall in love with?"

She tensed up her face.

"Will there be anything else, sirs?"

"Just the check," Dryden said. The waitress turned and left.

"Are you from another planet?" Dryden said. "That's not how you do things. It's a feeling you have to find on your own."

"We'll find a way."

"What the devil are you getting out of this? After all of this what are you getting out of this? Have you felt any enjoyment?"

Soames sat back in his chair.

"I can tell you that I enjoy it when you are having a good time, when you show enjoyment, vicariously. That's the only way. But nothing to make me enjoy an experience on my own other than through another person. I filmed you, you know? During your trysts with the prostitutes."

"What?" Dryden was incredulous. "You parasite. You son-of-a-bitch." He started to get up from the table.

"Don't worry. I didn't jack off — I believe that's the term — to your moaning and groaning."

"Why am I here? I'm done. I'm finished. You're worse than a voyeur. You're a pervert."

"I do have feelings, my boy. They are just buried, deeply buried."

"Why?"

"When I reach them I'll let you know why. Until then I'll double your per diem. Does that satisfy you?"

Just then the waitress came over and handed Dryden the check. He sat back down, looking at it on both sides. He began to smile.

"What is it now, Pete?"

"Her phone number," he said, sporting a Cheshire Cat's grin, holding the check up to Soames's face. "Dinner's on me tonight, you dick."

Part III

Soames was sitting in the dark when Dryden came back to his apartment.

"How did it go?"

"What the … ? … What are you sitting in the dark for? You scared the piss out of me."

Dryden turned on the light in the squalid Manhattan apartment he had lived in for the last four years.

"Did you enjoy that? Getting the piss scared out of you?"

"No."

"People pay money to go to movies that do that. I never understood the concept."

"Neither did I."

"So … how did it go?"

"It was only a first date. These things take time."

"Did you feel anything?"

"After about the third vodka tonic, yes."

"You wanted to sleep with her?"

"Sure. It would have been no problemo. But I wasn't in love with her."

"How long do you think this will take?"

"You can't put a stop watch on this, Soames. It either is or it isn't."

"I don't have much time, I must say."

"What do you mean?"

Soames handed him a green manila folder.

"It's a medical report. I have colon cancer. Apparently too much red meat and poor diet over the years, my doctor said. The Cubans didn't help much either."

"I'm sorry. I'm really sorry. Damn it. What are you going to do?"

"Nothing. Don't feel bad. I have access to pain medication. I'm not going to be cut open. Nature will take its course."

Dryden lowered his head.

"I'm sorry. After all you've done for me."

"In spite of our differences?"

"In spite of our differences. You have to admit, you're not an easy man to get along with."

"Agreed."

"What do we do?"

"We go on. As before. You continue to court this woman. Or any other. I have several months, maybe more."

"Maybe less. You don't know."

"The clock is meaningless. It's a short trip if you live to be a hundred. All that matters to me is whether you will fall in love or not."

Dryden sat down, took off his shoes, loosened his tie.

"I don't think it will happen with this woman."

"Who then?"

"I don't know," he said sternly. He got up from the sofa, went over to a tray with bottles of liquor sitting on a small table near a round mirror. He poured himself a Scotch and dropped some ice cubes in the glass.

Dryden sat back down and they both languished in silence for several minutes.

"Someone from your past?" Soames offered.

"What?" he said in mid gulp.

"Someone you once loved and that got away, or did not reciprocate."

"Go on," Dryden said in a dismissive tone.

"No. There was, wasn't there?"

"I suppose." Dryden finished his drink, got up, poured another, and then sat down.

"Tell me," Soames demanded. Dryden stared at the medical report on the glass table between them.

Part IV

Soames found her address and dug out the details from a private detective. They sat in Soames's limo outside her apartment. He read from the report the detective gave him.

"Rebecca Turner. Twenty-seven. Unmarried. No children."

"Give me that report," Dryden said, snatching it away. He read all four pages. "This tells me nothing. This doesn't tell me if she still has any feelings for me or not."

"You broke the engagement off?"

"Yes."

"Why?"

"I had an affair with someone else. I was stupid. I felt that I was getting married and I needed a fling to make up for all the things I missed in my life. Okay, Dr. Freud?"

"Don't be sarcastic. It does not become you."

"It's too late to go back. She'd never forgive me."

"I'll arrange something. She works at SellTec, an Internet company. I'll get you a job there."

"You can do that?"

"My boy," Soames said, as if that was enough.

"What will I do there?"

"You have a background in computers. I'll get you something as a systems analyst trainee, only you won't need to be trained. Get the picture?"

"I don't understand."

"You show up for work and everything else is taken care of for you. Can it be any more plain and simple?"

"I guess. You know best."

"I do."

Part V

Soames gave Dryden an apartment in his building, and increased his per diem to $1,000 per day.

Over the next several weeks Dryden showed up at SellTec and reacquainted himself with Rebecca, who was surprised to see him after such a long time. She even accepted a lunch invitation the first day he started work. He waited a few days, then asked her out on a formal date. She accepted. Dryden began to feel the old pangs return, and reported to Soames every day on his progress. But it felt very weird, almost like he was being set-up. Soames was growing visibly gaunt and weaker. Dryden decided to have a talk with him about the situation.

"I can't go on like this. You have to loosen the leash."

"The leash?"

"Yes. I can't keep talking to you about this every day. It's killing the feelings I have for her. I have to let this develop gradually. It's like if you have a plant ..."

"I completely understand, my boy. Go. Take your time. I won't interfere. When you're ready, you can come to me. Think of me as a friend. Can you pretend to do that?"

"I'd need to know your first name to do that."

"Bentley. Just don't call me Bent." Soames didn't bat an eyelash, but Dryden succumbed to laughter.

"You found that amusing?"

"I did. I did."

"Good. Very good. We are making good progress."

In the next month Rebecca and Dryden consummated their desires and two weeks later they were engaged. By this time Soames was turning into a shell of his former self. His apartment had been turned discretely into a hospice. Nurses dressed like secretaries, wearing tight skirts, black stockings, and stiletto heels; they cared for him around the clock. Doctors who dressed like business executives came in every day to check up on him. The pain medication made him groggy, but his mind was still as sharp as ever.

"How do you feel, Bentley?" Dryden said, leaning over the monstrous hospital bed, which resembled a large couch.

"I've been better. How are you, Pete?"

"Fine. Fine. This must be costing you a pretty penny?"

"What's the saying — you can't take it with you?"

"Always the card," Dryden said, smirking.

"I seem to amuse you. Good."

"Not at first. You kind of grow on people."

"How is everything with Rebecca?"

"We're going to be married next June."

"Wonderful. Remind me to attend."

"You're first on the list."

"Are you in love, Pete?"

"Yes."

"What's it like? To be in love?"

And Pete described it to him in the best way he could. After which Soames seemed pleased.

"Pete, I want you to know that my estate, what is remaining of it, will go to you when I die. A lawyer will contact you with the details."

"Always with the details," Pete said, a tear coming to his eye. "You're so good with details."

"That's where life is all about, the details and what's in them."

"I don't know what to say."

"Don't say anything. You have conducted yourself well. What you have done for me is beyond any monetary value. Pete, you have made me a very happy man. It has been a pleasure to have been your friend."

Soames raised his thin right arm and extended his boney fingers in order to shake Pete's hand. Pete was crying now; the tears were streaming. He shook Soames's hand. His grip was tight, then limp. A nurse came by to take his pulse. Bentley Soames was dead.

Peter Dryden left the apartment for the last time, went downstairs, hailed a cab, and then took it to Rebecca's apartment. That night he would tell her in guarded terms about his friend, and how he had brought happiness to Pete's life.

Part V (alternate ending)

"How do you feel, Bentley?" Dryden said, leaning over the monstrous hospital bed, which resembled a large couch.

"I've been better. How are you, Pete?"

"Fine. Fine. This must be costing you a pretty penny?"

"What's the saying — you can't take it with you?"

"Always the card," Dryden said, smirking.

"I seem to amuse you."

"Not at first. You kind of grow on people."

"How is everything with Rebecca?"

"We're going to be married next June."

"Wonderful. Remind me to attend."

"You're first on the list."

"Are you in love, Pete?"

"Yes."

"What's it like? To be in love?"

And Pete described it to him in the best way he could. After which Soames seemed pleased.

"Pete, I want you to know that my estate, what is remaining of it, will go to you when I die. A lawyer will contact you with the details."

"Always with the details," Pete said, a tear coming to his eye. "You're so good with details."

"That's where the devil is, so they say, in the details."

"Only you're not the devil. Far from it."

"Pete, I want you to be happy. Happier than anytime in your life."

"I am. I don't know what to say."

"Don't say anything. You have done all you could. What you have done for me is beyond any monetary value. Pete, you have made me a very happy man. It has been a pleasure to have been your friend."

Soames raised his thin right arm and extended his boney fingers in order to shake Pete's hand. Pete was crying now; the tears were streaming. He shook Soames's hand. His grip was tight, and grew tighter. Dryden couldn't break free. Suddenly the lights flickered. Dryden felt as if his life was being sucked out of his body — and it was. His last thoughts were of Rebecca. Pete Dryden slumped to the ground, dead.

Soames, looking twenty years younger, jumped up from the bed. Two nurses dressed him. Several bodyguards removed Pete Dryden's body, which had turned into an ashen rag carcass devoid of any life.

Soames looked at the mirror, adjusted his tie and led the two nurses out of the apartment.

"It never fails. It gets them every time."

A slight smile creased his lips.

The Low Self-Esteem Seminar

Now, I know a lot of you people have paid good money to be here today, so I'm not going to candy-coat it for you. I'll try and be brief so I can get out of here and start spending that hard-earned money of yours.

(mild laughter from the audience)

I'm being honest. All those self-help books you read did not help. They weren't supposed to help. That's why you're all here — to find out why they don't. They were supposed to make money for the author. That's why. I'm no exception. I'm here to make money. Only after this seminar you will not want to take another. There will be no follow-up, or workbook, or audiotapes, or $1,000 gift certificate off your $5,000 seminar next August in Maui. You must ask yourself — why do these guys who write these self-help books write more than one book? Some of them have six, eight, ten books — with more coming. Couldn't they get it right the first time? Of course not. Because they make money. And they want to make more. These books make people feel good — for a short time. And the more books you buy the more they will write. Hell, it beats working. I'm not here to delude you. I'm here to set you free. After today you're on your own.

Some of these books teach you to be grateful. That's okay. But, what exactly are you grateful for? Not that it isn't nice to give to charity in order to feel grateful, but what good did grateful ever get you? How many times have you heard about people on humanitarian missions who died in a plane crash? What was going through their minds as the plane was going down? Maybe they said, "Shit, I should have stayed home and watched reruns of Seinfeld."

Let's cut to the chase. Death. The Big D. See how that segues in nicely. You hear people say, "I want to die a peaceful death, and I want to die happy." Does it matter? You're dead. You will never know. You can't look back and say, "Boy, I had a good life." You can't look back. You don't know how your kids will turn out. Your wife may get remarried to an asshole. You will not know. That's not up to you. You think you'll be looking down from above through a skylight? And what's this *It's a Wonderful Life* crapola. That's for others to say. And are you living for others?

You've heard the old expression: "If you want to make God laugh, tell him what you're doing tomorrow."

(laughter)

True. True. But — suppose there is no God. Then who's laughing? We can't be sure. We can't be sure.

Now you're probably thinking I'm an atheist. No, I'm not technically an atheist. I'm an agnostic. There's a difference. Since we took your cell phones and their 900,000 apps and your wireless laptops and computers away before the seminar began (and left you with nothing but a note pad with real paper, a pen and your own brainpower), you will have to look up the difference after the seminar.

I'll spare you the suspense. An atheist is certain there is no God. An agnostic is uncertain. I'm not certain. I don't know. Why are we forced to choose? And if you choose God, there are a lot of choices after that.

Look. Life is a mystery, a wonderful, terrible mystery. No one knows. Anyone who pretends to know the answer is a fool. I don't know. I could be wrong. This is just my opinion based on my experience. But truth is not always subjective. This is just a way to cope until the answer comes along. It is a method of psychological survival. More on this later.

Just think about all the times you walked around and said "I'm turning over a new leaf," and the new leaf looks the same as the old one. It shrivels up and dies like all the others. You want something to get you through the day. You want to be happy. Happiness. What is happiness? Can it be sustained? I don't think it exists. Well, maybe for a few moments. Does it do you any good being optimistic? How many things really worked out well for you in your life. If things were working you wouldn't be here tonight, would you?

(scattered applause)

Let's look at the opposite. Being miserable. Being pessimistic. You spend most of your life being miserable, so how's that like? You hate your job, your marriage, your kids, the choices you've made in your life.

You can always count on something bad to happen. It's not the same with something good. You can do a million things right in your life, but one mistake can cost you everything. You can go to church on Sunday, raise a family, start a business, pay your taxes without cheating, and one day, something will happen to take it all away. You may get caught having an affair with a sixteen-year-old. Good-bye. You may lose your temper and accidentally knock someone over and in a freak of nature they drop dead. Sayonara. You pick up something in a store and walk out without paying for it. You get caught and your reputation goes out the window. You get into a fight with someone and they're injured. Suddenly you have a criminal record and you limit your options for any future endeavors. You declare bankruptcy. Suddenly you can't find a job. It can all change in an instant. You can spend your life climbing a mountain. All you have to do is slip up once. Fare thee well.

If you presume the worst, and something good happens, then you be surprised, and thus be more appreciative. Victory from the ashes of defeat, so to speak. Truth, as I've said, is hard to fathom. Honesty, however, is not. If you are honest with yourself you will have better time at dealing with life. You don't need any graphs, or steps, or tools — just be honest. Except when a lie will get you out of trouble.

(laughter)

Hope for the best and you will always be disappointed because life ends badly. Once you are dead you are dead. No matter what type of life you have lived you will be just as dead as the next person. So, don't be afraid to be depressed. Don't be ashamed of self-pity, laziness, and lack of motivation. These are all virtues. Embrace failure.

I admire the people who commit suicide. There is no finer commitment, no truer act. You are sick, you don't want to burden your family, or wind up in a hospital with a tube up your nose, so you end it. What's wrong with that?

(scattered applause)

Now, as for morality. Whatever you do in your life you must be able to live with yourself, you must accept the consequences. That's why we have laws. People are animals. We have laws to protect ourselves from ourselves. Some people say we don't have enough laws. Some people say we have too many laws. If you think we have too many laws, and want to get rid of them, go move to Somalia.

In your old age (if you are lucky) you look back on your life and you say, "Those were good times. Those are good memories." But, are they really? Is that really the way things happened? Recollections are at best an approximation. One can never know the truth about anything. That's why eyewitnesses in court are so easily discredited.

Now we come to family. You have children because you want to have something to outlive you. Bull. They are going to suffer and die just like you. Maybe it will turn out worse for them. And you brought them into the world to continue the cycle of misery.

Don't be afraid. Death does not exist. There is nothing beyond our knowledge. What makes us tick? I'll tell you. The Soul. And the Soul does not die.

(applause)

As for Fate and Destiny, they don't exist. Life is just a series of arbitrary events. There is no Master Plan. You could be dead tomorrow. I can drop dead right now on this stage.

You see people suffer as you sit home and complain about the weather. What an imbalance exists in the world. Children get cancer. Why? Part of a Master Plan my asshole. There is no Master Plan. We are all day-to-day.

Once you realize this and take it all in then you are free, free to live, free to make mistakes. You are not cursed. Neither are you being guided.

So, go forth. Be miserable. Fail, fail again, fail better, as Beckett said. Be happy in your misery. Because it all does not matter. Be paranoid, because they are out to get you. Dali said he encouraged his paranoia because it fueled his art. Art in itself is useless. It serves no purpose. Does it inspire you? Inspire you to do what? Maybe it inspires you to give up art once you realize you cannot create anything beautiful. Take solace in the fact that you cannot change anything. It all means nothing. Once you realize that then the pressure to achieve is over. You're free.

(applause)

Life is a mystery. Embrace it. We are all doomed.

(rousing applause)

Good night.

The Monarchs of Id

Preface

James Richard Hayden first came into contact with the Monarchs of Id one day as he was pruning his roses; a sudden and violent storm passed through our town and interrupted his activities. The wind kicked up and blew his skin back, spinning Hayden into a maelstrom that lasted seconds but seemed like hours. He was knocked unconscious. When he woke he had a revelation; looking at the sky it was as if a door had opened, revealing another world, a world past the dome of the sky, ruled by a consortium of power mongers who controlled history, down to the last decisive action. Something had tapped into his consciousness.

The challenge for him, he told me, was knowing if he was a willing participant in their plan, a puppet groomed by the masters, or if he was a variable that could somehow change history by some rebellious act.

Hayden told me this during one of our therapy sessions. He had been my patient for the past seven years and I was treating him for depression with a modicum of success. He wasn't dangerous, but he was not the type of person to be given to flights of fancy, green fairies, or sword and sorcery sagas.

After the "event" — as he liked to call it — I noticed a change in him. His speech was slightly altered, he had a more reserved appearance, and his knowledge of history became more acute. There were things he mentioned in detail that I had not remembered since my university days, historical minutiae, literary observations tied to quantum physics. It got so that after our sessions I would have to consult my online library to sift through his meanderings. After a while I cut back on my clients to give my exclusive attention to Hayden and his postulations on the design behind history, a design shaped by a group of controlling figures called the Monarchs of Id.

"The Monarchs make the Illuminati look like a chess club," Hayden told me.

Apparently, everything I knew or thought I knew to be true was not. Everything was planned, from the Civil War to the Kennedy assassinations to 9/11. Even the presidential elections and the Supreme Court appointments, right down to the actors chosen for movie roles (I often suspected this — how else could certain mediocre actors like George Clooney have a career?). It wasn't all hazard or whim. There was a plan, a mosaic, and Hayden was capable of seeing the puzzle pieces, the connections, and what was beneath the skin.

"The times you see things and shake your head and say: *This can't be possible* is when the mask is slightly lifted. Everything is under control. Everything is IN control."

I was meeting Hayden three times a week, devoting the rest of my time to research. Once I had a sizeable chunk of facts in my possession, I could begin to summarize and examine my findings. The sessions lasted as long as Hayden wanted them to last. I only billed the insurance company for an hour a week, least someone get suspicious. Hayden's paranoia was beginning to rub off on me.

The primary thought for me remained: When I found out what this was all about, what would I do? To paraphrase Chico Marx: "How am I gonna find out what I wanna find out when he no tell me what I wanna find out." Humor has often helped me through the anguish of two divorces and my teenage son's suicide. It helped me enormously here. Because I use it does not mean I trivialize my subject, patient, or my findings.

It was all unknown. John Lennon said that in an interview once. Hayden said that Lennon was on to the Monarchs, which is why he was murdered. Dylan was bribed (or threatened) to keep his mouth shut.

These are the sessions, transcribed verbatim by myself, copied and sealed in various locations throughout the world. If you are reading this that means a copy has made it into the world, the outer world, not the "world under the skin" as Hayden referred to it. I can only hope that it has made a difference and someone can piece together the puzzle.

The World Under the Skin: Part I
James Richard Hayden
July 7, 2017

"How are you doing today, James?"

"I am well."

"Have you had any more insights recently?

"They don't stop. Since the event happened, it's as if I had blinders removed, or bandages taken off my sightless eyes."

"What can you tell me? Back up, first tell me why you believe you can trust me to share your knowledge."

"I can tell. It's like I have ingrown antennae. I can see a threat a mile off. For now, that is. Something may happen to change that."

"What, for instance?"

"Another event."

"Let's start with the Monarchs. When did they come into being?"

"Since the first history book was written. The Dead Sea Scrolls, the Rosetta Stone, the Bible. Early cuneiforms. Centuries. Many centuries."

"How did they get here? Where does their power come from?"

"They were highly evolved beings that just found each other. They developed physics before there was physics, chemistry before there was chemistry. They found the DNA sequences when people on this planet were living in caves. They were able to find the right mates to help them evolve further. It was a quick process for them. The rest of the world took a long time catching up."

"Why not aid the evolutionary process along?"

"They did, but only for a select few. You see, they think of us as their pets. They observe us and in a way this tells them what not to do. But we're starting to catch up. We're still a long way off the evolution scale, but we're getting there. That's one of the reasons they had to stop the Nazis, they were getting close to genetic manipulation. Had to squash the competition. Anytime anyone gets too close they have to be contained. Every time the space program gets close to finding life on other planets their funding gets cut. They couldn't stop the atom from being split. Too many scientists had the knowledge."

"Is there life on other worlds?"

"Of course."

"Have the Monarchs contacted them?"

"Of course. Like I said. Competition. It's like an interplanetary Cold War. If the Monarchs are ever defeated, then the aliens will invade and take over. This is why I have mixed feeling about the Monarchs."

"Do you believe them to be malevolent or benevolent — in the long run?"

"Hard to tell. I hope the latter."

(end of session — to be continued)

Donald J. Gavron

The Minister of Sadness

The self-proclaimed "Minister of Sadness" bought a single red rose from a street vendor one rainy afternoon.

He brought it home to his apartment near the railroad tracks, on the outskirts of town, and kept the rose in a clear vase for as long as possible, until it withered and died.

He took the rose and had it cremated, then put the ashes in a tiny custom-made cedar coffin, lined with purple velvet. He sealed it up with glue.

The gold nameplate on the lid of the miniature coffin had an etching on it of a rose and the words:

Rose #1,957

The Minister of Sadness then placed it on a shelf in his den containing the other coffins filled with all the ashes of all the other roses he had bought over the years.

Three Guys Walk into a Bar ...

A surrealist, a dadaist and a nihilist all walk into a bar. The bartender asks them what they're drinking.

The surrealist asks for a glass of vodka with a cow's eyeball in it, and a straight razor on the side.

The dadaist asks for a bottle of Paris air, no chaser.

The nihilist doesn't want anything. He just stopped by to kvetch.

In the back room there's an existentialist going up and down a wooden ramp, loading and unloading the same case of Glenfiddich from a delivery truck.

Just then an anarchist bursts into the bar and sets off a bomb.

Everyone is killed except for the bartender, who is an absurdist.

He surveys the wreckage and says: "Now this is beginning to make sense."

Dead Words and More Weird Stories

Donald J. Gavron

Coal Miner's Elephant

My elephant was sick, so I took him to the vet. The waiting room was crowded that day. A diabetic dog, a fox with HIV, a wolf spider with a snake caught in its throat, a squirrel with one nut, a myna bird with a split lip (do they have lips?).

Anyway, my elephant, Andy, was having trouble peeing, so I wanted him checked out. He was leaking all over the place, he couldn't control himself. After all there's nothing much worse than stale elephant piss in your car. It always reminds me of my circus days.

I had to take a half-day off at the coal mine. The boss didn't seem too pleased.

"We've got a ton of bituminous just waiting there, just WAITING there!"

"Bituminous this," I said, flipping him the bird. "My elephant comes first. Do you have any idea what we've been through?"

"No, tell me Mr. Billionaire Bill Gates."

"Well. When I was in the circus we had a high wire act. Me, Andy, and Chelsea the hippo. The people used to come out in droves. They couldn't wait to see the act. First of all, they didn't believe that a hippo could do a triple back flip and

169

that an elephant could catch her with his trunk. It was incredible. We were the toast of the town.

"Then Chelsea started having an affair with Bernie the gorilla. Things went from bad to worse. Bernie used to beat her, and he was always throwing shit at her. Eventually it began to compromise the act. Bernie wanted to manage Chelsea, and all of a sudden her asking price went up. She was making more than me and Andy combined. Then she found out Bernie was fooling around with a cheetah. It wasn't pretty after that.

"We had a show at 6 p.m. one day and the crowd was juicy. The owner had dollar signs sewed onto his eyeballs.

"Then, during one of Chelsea's routine exchanges on the wire, she deliberately let go of Andy's trunk and landed smack dab on Bernie (who was in the audience with his cheetah), crushing him to death. Chelsea died of internal injuries some time later. It was a typical murder-suicide. Before she died she said to Andy: "Andy, you were my only true love." Andy went into a deep depression after that. That was it for the act.

"We wandered around for a while. Andy even tried to learn the saxophone. He got quite good at it, but there just wasn't any call for sax playing elephants, so I took this job in the mine to support us. But the elephant is everything to me, you see? Can't you see?"

"All right. All right. But we got all this bituminous ... Well, okay. I can see it means a lot to you. Go ahead. But hurry back. I still have a business to run." Just then the boss reached back and dredged up a big black loogie that he fired off into the sunset.

After an hour in the waiting room, the doctor took a look at Andy and prescribed some black powder to mix in with some pomegranate juice. The doctor was a little Chinese man who was suspected of selling organs and stale ostrich eggs on the black market. He stared at me through thick-lensed glasses.

"Three times a day. Four times on Sunday. See you in two weeks."

We went back home to watch the Discovery Channel

and reconfigure our plans for the future.

Andy took the recliner and I lay on the floor because of my bad back.

"What are we going to do?" I asked.

"That son-of-a-bitch is going to be mad at you," Andy said, opening a bottle of Glenmorangie. "That's all I know."

"I don't care. I just don't care anymore."

I heard him snicker behind me, the leather recliner squeaking, rocking, squeaking, rocking.

"C'mon, man. The future is ours. The future is bright."

He took a big swig from the bottle.

"Don't forget your pomegranate juice, and the medicine the doctor gave you, " I told Andy.

"That guy was a quack. I don't even think he was Chinese."

"I'm just trying to take care of you, that's all."

"You do right, you do right."

"I guess we'll have to move on — again. The hobo life."

"You have a plan?"

"I'm working on it," I said. I was staring at the ceiling like it was a star map, my back in a rage.

"You da man," Andy said with a snort, laughing hysterically, his trunk wrapped around his bottle of Glenmorangie. "You da man! Hobo life here we come!"

There's no reasoning with a drunken elephant.

Dream Stations

"Dreams are at times but reflections of emotions, not real events; or they are projections of possible real events, and the accompanying emotions. They are more than detritus — they are expressions of a deeply hidden emotional state."
— Dr. Curtis B. Strickland, Ph. D., NCPsyA, Parkhouse University, Berlin, New Hampshire

I am walking around what looks like a coliseum, or ballpark, or non-secular university. I realize that it is the Steve McQueen Memorial University, dedicated to his work for some church he had been involved with prior to his death from cancer at age 50.

McQueen was one of my heroes. A digital projection of him speaking suddenly appears (in black-and-white), right over the entrance to the structure.

"Do anything you can without hurting anyone else. Use fear or intimidation if you have to, but only against yourself, to achieve your dreams," McQueen said. "Thank you. This is Steve McQueen."

Then his wife appears, projected also, sobbing, begging people for donations to keep the university running. But not just for the university, for all the people it would help.

The scene changes. An old girlfriend named Sarah stands next to me, holding my hand. We were walking outside a New York baseball stadium in summer. People are cheering.

Sarah is 22, the age when I first knew her. Her hair is short and red, her eyebrows dark and imposing, arching over her sad eyes, her pale face sprinkled with freckles. She is dressed in a tight, black full-body swimsuit; a towel is wrapped around her waist. She has open-toe sandals on.

"Are we going to the beach?" she asks.

"Yes," I say. "Yes."

Then we are at Sandy Hook, New Jersey, lying on towels on a concrete slab that used to be the base of a lifeguard station overlooking the beach and the ocean. We are close enough from the other people to hear them, but far enough away not to let it bother us. The sun is burning hot.

She's staring at the water, her body draped like a panther across the towel, her legs extended like Cleopatra on a barge floating down the Nile. I am applying suntan lotion to her shoulders and her exposed back. As I do this I count the freckles on her white skin, I run my fingers along her shoulder blades, and down her spine.

"This is heaven, isn't it," she asks. "At least for this moment. It will never happen again."

"A slice of heaven," I say, and she turns to look at me askance, her eyes inviting me to seduce her.

The page turns. Now I'm driving in a car with my ex-wife Sandra past a glass house in the countryside. It was an architect's building, and there were tiny offices on each of the three floors. Sarah was in the glass house, on the third floor, facing the road, in one of the lighted offices, standing at a desk full of architectural drawings. She's crying. She's wearing a black business suit with a bright white shirt open at the collar.

Sandra and I drive back to our apartment where she shows me all the letters and cards and photos Sarah and I had exchanged over the years.

"I want you to burn these. I want you to tell me you are finished with her."

"I can't," I say quietly.

"Then I'm leaving," she says, swiping her hand at the pile of memorabilia and knocking the correspondence and photos to the floor. All the cards and letters are white, some covered with glitter. They light up the room.

I blink and I'm somewhere else. I'm in Joyce's car now. Another old girlfriend, albeit a brief one. She was thin and had dark hair and she had the bronzed tan skin of an athlete. At one time she was a ballet student, then a teacher. She's searching for a joint in her glove compartment, then finds it and puts it in her mouth. We're driving alone on a coast highway. It's raining and the canopy of trees all seem like they're about to reach out and grab us.

She lights the joint and passes it to me like a baton and now we're in some race for life or death. The air grows heavy and my head grows light and suddenly we are in the bedroom of her apartment and she's stripped down to her black lace underwear. The place is a mess. She notices that I notice and says, "Little bit of heaven, isn't it?" Then she removes her bra. Her white tits are sagging slightly, but they are voluptuous.

We're about to go at it and her phone rings. It's an old black rotary phone. Her old boyfriend, just out of prison, is on the other end and he's at the airport and he wants her to pick him up.

"We don't have much time," she tells me. I'm staring at the nipples reflected in her eyes. "Let's do it."

I open my eyes. A group of us are at a resort in the Bahamas. On the hot bright beach, people are taking pictures. I'm with my family — my nieces and my nephew and their parents, and an ex-girlfriend named Anaïs. Her hair is golden blonde. She's wearing a straw hat and laughing. She has on round black sunglasses and I can't see her eyes. But she's smiling, laughing, and obviously very happy. I seem to remember that I was happy with Anaïs, but then something happened. I don't have the nerve to ask her what it was.

In the shower stalls on the beach they're showing a clip from *True Grit*, the John Wayne film. It's the famous shoot out at the end. I've seen the film a dozen times.

I yell out to everyone from around the corner of the stalls: "Come and watch this, it's John Wayne! Come on!" But they're too busy laughing and taking pictures. Besides, John Wayne is dead. He's been dead for a long time. Just like McQueen.

I turn around and I'm in a candy store in a small town in Pennsylvania. There are barrels filled with black licorice for sale. The walls are covered with cheap toys wrapped in cardboard and plastic, the type of stuff you wouldn't sell but only give away. Jars filled with candy lined the counter top — caramels, lemon-drops, orange taffy, and chocolate-covered cherries. An old soda fountain station with round red-cushioned chairs stood empty in a far corner of the store. Some of the chairs were torn, and the gray stuffing was peeking out. Kids were spinning them.

"Can I interest you in some licorice?" the young girl behind the counter asks. She doesn't look familiar to me.

"Can I get a map? Or at least an address?"

"I'm afraid we don't have any maps. And there is no address."

"How will I find my way back here?"

"Do you want to come back, after everything that's happened?"

I think about that one for a while.

Now it's winter solstice. The ground is covered with snow. I'm alone in an old Victorian house that is lavishly decorated. I've noticed that in most of my dreams the houses are sparsely furnished, or empty. Not this time. This time it's different.

In the parlor there are leather couches and cherry wood curio cabinets containing porcelain figurines. Lace doilies are placed strategically on end tables holding crystal candy dishes filled with red licorice and ribbon candy. Thick velvet drapes with gold braids cover the windows. Oil lamps light the rooms with a dim flicker. An oak staircase, polished to perfection, stands imposingly near the front entrance. The rooms are decorated with stained glass windows, flowery wallpaper, and antiques. A brick fireplace is crackling with burning cedar planks. I am soaking up every detail.

Through a tiny window in the corner of the parlor I can glimpse the yard. Someone is shoveling snow in the distance. A cardinal rests on the naked branch of a tree. A frozen clothesline is sagging between two rusted poles. A dog is running through the snow backwards, jumping up in the air, trying to snag some unseen treat.

A shadow leads me to a waiting room, just off the parlor. A tiny chandelier hangs overhead. I sit down on a cameo-backed settee and begin to hear the voices of my past. The room is warm and I am comfortable. I realize finally that I am here to help the dead people from my past to their next level, their next station. Someone will be along soon to tell me precisely what to do. I know I will be here for quite some time.

Dear Meteor

So I'm outside last night about eleven o'clock looking into the sky and trying to see some meteors. The news broadcast said there would be a meteor shower, so I believed them. I've never seen a meteor streak across the sky, and it doesn't look like I'll be seeing one this nochy. Staring into the vast expanse of night I see the stars come into focus the longer I watch. I'm sort of in the country, not in the city, but there are streetlights along the road playing with my vision. The sky is clear and beautiful; some planes fly by, the stars twinkle twinkle, but where the hell are the meteors? I think I see one or two in my peripheral vision, but maybe they're only floaters from the back of my eyeballs. I go inside and try to find my binoculars. I can't find them. Where the hell are they? No use. Back outside. Looking. Looking. Cars drive by in the darkness lighting up the road. Then I hear what sounds like a bicycle with a flat tire coming down the sidewalk, but it isn't a bicycle. Through the pine tree in front of my house it looks like someone jogging with a dog. I look again. Several deer are crossing the road and walking along the sidewalk towards the tennis courts. They stop under the light. Here come some more. Five. Six. Then two small ones jogging. Seven. Eight. They run past the tennis courts and into the woods behind it. One lone buck stands there under the street light in the parking lot, staring back at me. I make a subtle noise and tell him to shoo. *Go. Go ahead. Go in the woods and be safe. Go.* It runs away, then turns a corner near the tennis courts and runs into the temporary safety the patch of woods offers. I think to myself: How can anyone hunt a deer? One of God's most harmless creatures. Why? But they do. Sport. Sport, my ass. What goes on in a mind like that I don't want to know. There is no room for compromise in my mind. This is unacceptable. And I go back inside thinking what a beautiful but messed up world this is. But it isn't really the world, it's the people in it. And I still haven't seen one damn meteor.

Donald J. Gavron

Franz Back from the Grave

"Franz, how does it feel to be back?"

"I'm looking at all this palaver on the Internet and it just seems like a lot of self-indulgent whining. That's what it comes down to. Wailing banshees locked in a death grip; battling egos succumbing to their most horrific nature."

"Don't you feel a sense of community on the Net?"

"No. A bunch of spoiled, over- or under-educated buffoons who don't know a thing about syntax trying to correct each other in order to — what? — bring about an aesthetic stasis?"

"Aren't you being a little harsh?"

"Harsh? Life is harsh. The world is harsh. How many people are starving on and off the continent? And all everyone wants to know is if his or her putrid story is accepted or rejected by some idiotic Internet magazine. They aren't magazines, folks. If you can't get ink on your fingers when you read it then it isn't a magazine. Or a book. Or a pamphlet. These Internet books have no spine."

"This is the new way. Things change."

"To hell with the new way. A parade of idiots in lockstep who have killed the written word. Books are obsolete. People can't learn anything on their own; they pilfer things from the Internet. They think everything is public domain. Actions have consequences. The written word is sacrosanct. When everyone starts to realize that, then there will be hope."

"Do you think plagiarism is rampant on the Internet?"

"By the time you find out something has been poached it has been used sixteen ways to Sunday. Look, I've given up writing. Why do you think writers give up writing and painters give up painting?"

"I don't know."

"Because they've had enough bullshit. Look at Rimbaud. He said everything he needed to say by the time he was twenty. When Hemingway found out he couldn't write he shot himself. Pure act of ego. But Rimbaud said what he had to say and he was done with writing. All writers should either stop writing when they're around twenty or else start when they are over sixty. When you are young you have all these grandiose notions of the world that are pure, from the soul. When you reach forty you know, or should know, what the world is all about. It is a vile, disgusting, hazardous place populated by selfish idiots looking for validation."

"What writers do you admire?"

"No writer likes to read another writer's work. It's like admiring someone else for fucking your girlfriend or boyfriend. They like their own voice. They want to do their own fucking. That's it. If they admire someone else it is just lip service. They don't really mean it."

"Is that the way you think about your work?"

"Every artist thinks he's God. An artist is a creator, held to his own standard. There's only room for one God in the universe. When someone comes along and attempts to fix him, to tell him something should be improved, that someone is incurring the wrath of God. How foolish is that? How foolish is the fool who attempts to get inside the writer's head and know what he wants to say and then dares to correct him?"

"What is writing all about then? Is it ego?"

"What else? Look at the writers who sacrificed

relationships, marriages, time with their children, their health, all to sit in a room and scribble on a piece of paper or pound away at a typewriter — I guess it would be a keyboard today. What the hell is so important that you can't take the time to be with your wife or children, or go to a dentist? Joyce ignoring his family, Fowles ignoring his stepdaughter, Mailer going through wives like Kleenex. It's selfishness, plain and simple. Nothing else in the world matters except their precious written word. And who reads what they write? Bumpkins."

"So, there is no one other than yourself that you admire?"

"I admire the man who invented the polio vaccine. He saved a lot of lives, probably a lot of writers also."

"Is there nothing the writer does that is useful?"

"Art — and I mean all art — is useless. It serves no purpose, except to keep the frame shops and moving companies and museum directors in business. If you got rid of all the art in the world, life would go on."

"But people yearn to create. The ancient cave dwellers painting on their walls. The primitives who banged on their drums. These were the pre-cursers to the artists of today."

"That person in the cave was not Mozart or Da Vinci. They used the drums to signal each other in case they were attacked. The paintings were a diary of their lives, a way of teaching others. This is survival. This is practical application."

"You can't believe that?"

"I know what I know. Look at all the people in the world who have never heard Mozart or read Shakespeare, except when they were forced to in school. Look at them! Are they better than you? Are they better than me? No."

"So, are you finished writing?"

"You bet your ass I'm not."

"But why? Why do you continue to write, after all that you just said."

"Because I'm God. No one can tell me differently."

"Thank you, Franz. Welcome back."

Warning — This Story May
Harm Your Computer

I had given up seriously trying to connect with people. Following all the social media protocols, I signed up with clubs, movements, causes, lists, message boards, ancestral archive searches, companion seekers, personal ads, job exchanges, literary and art appreciation societies — almost anything that stirred my imagination. One day I realized I had unwittingly signed up with both the NRA and the Jim Brady Society. I was receiving upwards of 500 e-mails a day. My time (which was taken up with too much drinking and pornography) was much too valuable to sacrifice. Suppose, God forbid, I got a job offer (I applied to all the proper job search agencies)? But I didn't.

It's a dull life being a prisoner of one's own mind, but it has some advantages. Three years ago I was laid off from the newspaper, and it's been over a year since my last unemployment check. I was living on the fumes left from my savings, in the attic apartment of my dead mother's Aunt Virginia, who is eighty-nine. Out of the goodness of her heart (as she reminds me more often than not) I am allowed to stay rent free in exchange for doing her shopping, running errands, taking her to church, etc. I was even enlisted to paint her porch and scrub her floors. When she asked me to do those things I could sense her studying my facial expressions for signs of protest, but I kept my cool. "Only too glad to do so, Auntie." I'd smile, she'd turn her back and walk away, and I'd grimace and flip here the finger. It wasn't as if she was cruel, but she was super strict and passive-aggressive to the nth degree. She found fault with everything I did. I folded my blanket the wrong way. I drank from the milk carton. Dirty shoes made her upset. Leaving the top off the orange juice container was enough to provoke a lecture on respect for others. She had no problem pointing out my transgressions. She wouldn't allow cable or satellite service into the house. "I won't let them to drill into my foundation." "Two tiny holes, Auntie?" "I don't care." And that was final.

Auntie Ginny (as I called her) intimated to me on more than one occasion that I'd be in line for an inheritance of some substantial amount when she met her maker. The day of that meeting could not come soon enough.

I dreamed of what I would do with the money, with any money. I'd fix my computer (or buy as new one), purchase (or lease, depending on the terms) a car, buy some clothes, have the cash to take a woman out on a date — I'd be able to do any number of things. I could be the person I wanted to be. Of what use was money to that old woman? She spent forty years working for the phone company. Her stock was worth a mild fortune. She had no children, no living relatives except for myself, which I think she regretted. She drove her husband to an early grave (probably from having him wash the floor and paint the porch regularly) when he was fifty-two. The more I thought about it the more it seemed like a good idea if she left this mortal coil.

Once a month she visited her doctor, whether she needed to or not. And guess who was elected to take her? I'd help her down the back stairs of the old three-story building she owned since the 1950s, and it would be such an easy task to simply trip her up and have her plunge down the rotten old steps to a probable and deserving death. That was the problem. It was probable. It wasn't guaranteed. If she survived (and the old bitch was almost certain to do so), I would be cooked. No inheritance, nothing to look forward to except jail time. On top of that I was a coward. I never took chances. That was a constant in my life. There had to be another way. I had nothing but time to think of one.

Once again, it wasn't as if she was a bad person, but she was a miserable one, and each day she survived was a day that prevented me from enjoying my life. One day, my Aunt provided me with the germinal of a plan. The car she owned, and on rare occasions allowed me to drive (a 1962 aqua blue Chevy Impala), refused to start as we readied ourselves for her appointment at the doctor. I left my Aunt at the top of the stairs when I went to start the car. "Don't move, I'll be right back," I said to her. My suggestions usually have the opposite effect on my Aunt, and this advice was no exception. When I finally started the car (it was flooded) and backed into the driveway, I saw her descending the stairs, cane in one hand, the other gripping the shaky wooden railing. I watched her lift her right leg, balance on her shaky left leg, and then plant her foot on the next step, like a goose step in slow motion. I sat and watched in a numb daze, hoping for a misstep, but it never came. Finally, her gaze caught mine. I feigned disapproval by shaking my head and leapt from the car, running up the stairs to meet her.

"Now, Aunt Ginny, you know you shouldn't be doing that. What if you fell?"

"I'm tired of waiting. Come on, help me."

A light went off. I put myself in a frame of mind that it would not be a terrible thing if she fell down the stairs. With this thought in place I became more mindful of the local weather report for the next several weeks and waited for the forecast of a rainstorm. When it rained the overhang onto the back stairs leaked during a heavy downpour. Not a great amount, but enough to coat some of the steps and make them slippery. That was the opening I needed.

I was nothing if not patient. Each indignity only heightened my interest in the nightly forecasts. A backed-up toilet — *clean it.* A wasp's nest near the telephone pole not near enough to the house to cause any danger — *get rid of it!*

A small coating of leaves on the back lawn — *rake them!* These were the indignities I was subject to. These were the things I had to look forward to in my life.

Her next doctor's appointment was for October 3rd, and the forecast that week was for intermittent showers. These weather people had been wrong before, but I clearly remember about a year ago when it rained and I had to wipe off the steps in order for my Aunt to walk down (with my arm wrapped around hers). It's funny how you don't recall these things when you are in a certain state of mind. Now walking was more difficult for her, and I formulated a plan to use her impatience and hardheadedness to my advantage.

On the morning of the 3rd a bright sun opened up beyond the thin clouds, and I feared my scheme would not be brought to fruition. I prayed for rain, but didn't think that appropriate. Then, fate intervened, as it always does. A mild rain began in the late morning, then escalated into the early afternoon. It was one o'clock and my Aunt's appointment was for two o'clock. I considered the hall and saw the tiny drips fouling the steps. Was it enough? I watched, and stared, and hoped. Each raindrop was my potential salvation; each wet spot was my escape from this hell. I waited as long as I could, until the old nag started to call out.

"Let's get ready. Get the car, nephew."

"I'm looking for the umbrella." I pretended to look.

"What's going on? We'll be late." Good. She was starting to get anxious.

"It must be in the car," I said in a tone low enough so that she would have difficulty hearing me.

"What? What did you say?"

I climbed the steps to get her. Helping her on with her coat I deliberately made it difficult for her to put her arm through. She was getting angry.

"Damn it all, can't you do anything right?"

Maybe I can, Auntie, maybe I can. I began to laugh inside at how things were proceeding according to my wishes. I was trying not to be over confident. At worst this would make a good test run for another time, but I hoped for the best.

I maneuvered her to the edge of the top of the staircase.

"Wait here. Don't move, or I'll be cross with you. I'm going to get the car and the umbrella and I'll be back to wipe off the steps. Don't move. You have to listen to me."

"Go on, you pup. Hurry it up. I'll be late."

I descended the stairs, carefully avoiding the wet spots. Wouldn't it be ironic if I was the one who fell? I was able to notice that enough moisture had accumulated to possibly cause an accident, but I wasn't certain. If my idea did work, fine. If not, then it was back to square one. I would find another way. Or maybe the old beast would just croak in her sleep. Before I went out the door, I yelled back to her.

"Make sure you listen to me and stay there." I knew this vexed her. She never listened to me. It was the cherry on top of my plan.

I ran into the street and waited in the car. The downpour was steady and the rain pounding on the roof was like sweet music to me. I waited. And waited. And waited. Surely she must be climbing down by now. When I thought enough time had passed, I went back, and, to my consternation, she was still standing at the top of the steps.

"What the hell is taking so long?" she bellowed.

She looked old and fragile and helpless. I almost felt sorry for her.

"The ... the car won't start again. Wait there. I'll get the umbrella."

"Let's call a cab. I can't wait any longer."

"Just a minute. Just a minute."

I was beside myself. Damn. Maybe it was not meant to be. Of all the luck. What's the old saying — "If it wasn't for bad luck I wouldn't have any"? That typified my situation. I backed the car up, and then waited some more, this time I was within view of the staircase. Still no Aunt Ginny. Then I saw a raised foot. Here she came, the old bitch, the old strong-willed coot. Choke on your money you old buzzard. Come on down. Just like "The Price is Right." Come on down. To your death. The light from a single dim bulb illuminated her impending demise. One step. Wait. Two steps down.

Wait. She didn't look over. She was concentrating. I could sense her determination. Nothing could hurt her, she was saying to herself. I am immortal. I will live forever. Nothing will prevent me from doing what I must do. That's it. Hurry. Hurry for your appointment. The fate of the world depended on it. Hurry. Third step down. It had to be wet there. I looked. Then, it happened. SQUEAK KA-THUMP BAM BAM BAM KA-THUMP BAM down the staircase she went. BAM. I heard the cane bounce on its way down. CRACK PING PANG BAM. THUMP. I think her head hit the concrete, but I wasn't sure, I had my hand over my eyes.

I felt bad. If only there was another way. If only she was a nicer person, I would have only been too glad to help her. If only she wasn't such an old stubborn miser. God rest her miserable soul.

Then the realization struck me like a hammer — suppose she survived the fall?

I got out of the car, carrying the umbrella. It would be my excuse. "I went back for the umbrella, officer." There were no witnesses. The house next door was deserted and for sale. My story would be beyond the slightest doubt. I stood the umbrella up in a corner of the stairwell, next to her still body.

I felt her pulse. Yes. The old witch was dead. She cracked her skull on the concrete at the bottom of the stairs. The rain, on cue, had dissipated by the time the ambulance had arrived, but it was too late to save her.

"She's dead, I'm afraid," the EMS worker said.

I had warned her. It wasn't as if I didn't. She did it to herself. My hands were clean. Sure, I probably could have prevented it, but why did I have to interfere? I suppose there were laws against indifference in knowing an accident could occur, but this did not fit in with my own view of morality. In my universe, there was only an obligation to myself, and I had told myself a long time ago that I had to be prepared to live with any decision I made in my life.

I rode to the hospital and tried to remain calm. I tried to act shaken, repeating my story for all to hear. "I told her to wait. She was a stubborn woman. I loved her so much." I couldn't cry, but I rubbed my eyes with my hands so that they appeared red. They seemed to buy it. The police eventually came and I made a statement. It all appeared to be tied up in a nice, neat little package. All I needed was the bright green ribbon to decorate it, the bright green ribbon made of money.

Just as I suspected, she left a great deal of her money to me (after the half million she left to her church), in a trust, but that was all right. She gave me the old house (which I sold) and a stipend of $2,500 a month (she had no idea of the cost of living) until I was sixty-five, when I would get the balance of the $1.2 million she had in her account (which my business advisor estimated would be between five and six million by that time). The profit from the sale of the old building came to $180,000, which I immediately placed into Certificates of Deposit (with some cash left over for me to indulge myself). It all came together. I was set for life. The outcome only gave me added confidence to pursue my dreams. I was not a greedy or ostentatious person, so I rented a nice apartment in town and lived moderately, unless I decided to connect with a young woman and take her out on the town. I donated the old Impala and leased a hybrid SUV. I bought a top of the line computer with all the programs, and took some courses in web design at the local community college. Things were going well.

One night I awoke in a sweat. I don't know why. Weeks passed. My classes were over, and I started my own business. There were no more bosses in my life. Clients began to find me. Money came in. I worked when I wanted to. There was no pressure in my life.

A few weeks later the sweats began again. I went to see a doctor and he pronounced me fit. Was it due to a guilty conscience, I wondered? Why? I was happier than I had ever been. If I went to a therapist I would never be able to explain what happened. Whatever I revealed would only lead to more sessions that would amount to nothing except my being diagnosed with a guilty conscience. I know I contributed to her death, but I didn't kill her. I could live with that.

One night, my computer (which was on a desk in a corner of my bedroom) came on. The blue light from the blank 24" screen filled the room. I reached for my glasses and tumbled out of bed. I was sweating again. Then something appeared on the screen. It was the web site I was building for a real estate client. There was a video playing, but it wasn't the video I created. It was a video of the back stairs of my Aunt's house the day she fell and died. Then I heard screams that I never heard before, and I heard bones cracking. It was my aunt falling. The fall seemed to take longer than it actually did. It was in slow motion. Then there was a close up of me in the car, laughing. I slapped my face. Was it a dream? No. I noticed on the screen a flashing button to the side of the video, a link to the local police station. All I had to do was press it and the video would be sent to them. Where did it come from? I tried to delete it, but couldn't. Instead, I unplugged the computer. It remained on, no doubt still running on the battery. I took a quick shower, dressed, and made my way to the corner bar, which was still open. I needed somewhere to hide until I could figure out what to do. After a few gin and tonics I couldn't take staring at the hockey game on the tube over the register, and the pot-bellied bartender was making me squeamish. So much for the local trashy nightlife. The drinks did not relax me, and I came up with no solutions for my dilemma.

When I returned, the computer was still on and the video was playing over and over on a loop. That was it. I had enough. I picked up the computer and walked down the stairs of my apartment and to my vehicle, depositing the monitor and hard drive in the back. It started to rain; a somber mist, and I made my way to the park near the lake in the town where I lived. I found a secluded spot and backed up near the lake, opened the hatch, and threw the computer off a short pier into the lake. It sank, the glow from the monitor still visible under the water, and I stood and watched until the glow disappeared.

Whether it was the mist from the rain or my profuse sweat, I arrived home drenched. I took off my clothes and dumped them on the floor. *Pick those up!* someone said, or I thought someone said. The refrigerator rattled. Maybe I was just hearing things. I took a hot shower, toweled off, and then put on some jogging pants and a t-shirt. When I was done I noticed that the computer was back, in its original spot, in the corner of my bedroom. I hadn't noticed it when I returned, or did I? Did I ever take it away? I wasn't sure. Walking slowly over to it I saw that it was running the same video of my Aunt Ginny falling down the stairs. I could have taken the computer away again, but I didn't bother. There was no use. I was trapped. I was still trapped in my Aunt's vengeful web.

I sat down and opened a word processing program and began to compose a letter. As I wrote it a strange thing happened. The font control was out of whack. The program took on a life of its own..

To Whom It May Concern:
My **name** is <u>Thomas Hollinger</u>.
On October 3rd, 20__, I was
<u>responsible</u> for my Aunt
Virginia Coleman's
<u>**death**</u> by <u>**my**</u> indifference
in watching her descend
<u>a</u> flight of
stairs as <u>**I**</u> was
waiting in my <u>car</u>
on a <u>rainy</u> day and about to
take **<u>her</u>** to her

doctor. I **deliberately** delayed **her** from going to the doctor until **she** became anxious and decided to walk **down** the steps <u>herself</u>, without my aid, which I always gave her. I did this to **inherit** her money.

I **didn't** mean to.
I <u>loved</u> my Aunt.
No. No, I <u>didn't</u>.
I <u>did</u> mean to **kill** her.
I <u>HATED</u> her.
I wanted her dead.
I threw
her
down the steps…
No!
I didn't mean to do it.

No.

I did.

I
did.

I killed
her.

I threw her down the steps.

<u>Yes</u>.

I
Killed HER.

*

God, Infinity, the Soul, and Edgar Allan Poe

I've been seeing the numbers 1234 (in that sequence) lately, showing up on the clock, the microwave, the car radio, the indicator in the corner of the television, anywhere a sequence of numbers can show up. Sure, it only happens on the clock twice in a day, but I seem to always key in on it in other ways also. I bought some things at the drug store the other day and the bill came to $12.34. There's was address to send away for a DVD — 1234 Bakersfield. I paused a long song I was listening to and it stopped at 12:34 on the counter. I thought this was more than coincidence. So, I grew inquisitive and did some numerology research.

I always thought an ascending sequence of numbers meant "going in the right direction," but that almost always seems to not be the case with me. Often I feel like I'm spinning my wheels or going backwards just a bit. Occasionally I do think I'm moving in the right direction, but maybe I have not been paying enough attention. I also came across this: "The numerology number 1234 is one of self-determination and independence. The number is especially good at discovering new ways to do things." After some more digging I found this: "You're on the right track and taking the right steps to elevate your vibration, further open your heart, integrate more of your higher spiritual truth and nature and make a positive change in your life and in the world." Wow.

Now, those that know me and know me well know that I am not one to believe in superstition. I'm not a believer in the Karmic wheel of things always working out or good things coming back to you. Reincarnation? Maybe. It's fun to think so anyway. But if there is anything I believe it is this: All things end and that they most often end badly. From the experience of losing people close to me, I know this to be the case. Everyone who has been emotionally close to me has suffered before they died. It's not like they were struck dead by a car, or had a stroke and died before they hit the floor, or died in their sleep. No. They lingered. They lingered in hospitals with tumors, or bleeding ulcers, or fevers, or some form of cancer that made them suffer restless nights and horrendous pain and frightening hallucinations. I'm not a believer in the "master plan." There's too much agony and suffering and death for me in the world to trust the cosmic universe to make everything all right. Not that I'm unhappy, I'm grateful. But I could be more happy. Everyone could.

It's all a matter of perspective. Things could be worse. They can always be worse. But they can be better also. I guess I'm never content. I think there might be something wrong with me if I was content all the time. Things change and not always for the better. I win some little battles now and then, but I want to win the war, or a few major battles before I join the dust.

Back to the numbers. There's also the number 123, a variation of 1234. I see 1:23 a.m. or p.m. (or other ways) a lot, but not as often as 12:34. 123 means: "You are being guided, and you are taking the right steps on your path, or maybe even to more fully realign with your highest path." God knows I need guidance, I just don't want to be conned (I must also note I never noticed the numbers in descending order — 321 or 432 or other descending sequences on the clock or elsewhere).

So, what do I believe in, you may ask? The Soul. Infinity. These are things I can't deny. I've tried, but I can't.

Edgar Allan Poe wrote a paper near the end of his life called "Eureka." It is a complex piece of writing, an essay on the make-up of the Universe — Truth, God, the Soul, Infinity — the usual beach-reading subjects. One of the things I remember is Poe's observation on God and Infinity. The gist of this essay (or prose poem, as Poe subtitled the work) is (I think): "If we cannot conceive of Infinity, how can we possibly conceive of God?" That struck me like an an ant getting hit with an anvil.

Poe goes on to say: "Nevertheless, as an individual, I may be permitted to say that I cannot conceive Infinity, and am convinced that no human being can."

He also quotes a philosopher, Baron de Bielfeld: "We know absolutely nothing of the nature or essence of God: — in order to comprehend what he is, we should have to be God ourselves."

The Soul has to exist. It must. Or maybe it doesn't. I hate to think I'll never know. If you get a chance, read "Eureka." You may think Poe was going insane as he wrote it, or you may think you are being enlightened as you read it — or are being driven insane as you begin to understand it.

But, whatever happens, I believe Poe was sincere in his beliefs, and his belief in God, as the final lines attest: "In the meantime bear in mind that all is Life — Life — Life within Life — the less within the greater, and all within the Spirit Divine."

Maybe I am on the right path. Maybe I'm being guided, either by myself or the universe or some unrecognizable spirit. The comedian George Carlin used to have a routine where he asked, "What's with all the angels? Where are the zombies? What happened to the zombies?" Well, George, there are a lot more zombies around today, some of them spiritual zombies, but most of them material. I don't want any part of those zombies. I just have to know if I am doing the right thing. But, right and wrong are self-evident. Maybe I want just a little guidance from the angels. Maybe I'm getting it. Or maybe I've had too much damn coffee — again!

The Purpose of Knowledge

The expedition commanded by Sir Arthur Youngblood was an arduous one expected to take many weeks searching the Himalayas until finally reaching the desired destination in Tibet, at the so-called "roof of the world."

Sir Arthur had long theorized that the secret to all knowledge was centered somewhere in Tibet. Years of meticulous research, failed endeavors, and a good portion of his family's wealth had gone into his obsession. Even though he was knighted by the Queen for his efforts in the war, this had merely been a formality; and his commission had seemed like an afterthought to the men at the Expedition Club he spent most of his retirement hiding in. He needed some test to give his life meaning. If he did not achieve something monumental in his life he would not die a happy man. After much thought and preparation, he began his journey to the highest point of the earth, with a company of twelve, in 1904.

Some of the men had been in his company in the Sudan, riflemen known for their strong stock and perseverance. Some had been veterans of the Boer Wars in South Africa. They were servants to the dwindling British

Empire, and many felt defeated and obsolete, although they would never show it. Their faces read like roadmaps to a graveyard of dying souls. He purposely chose men who had few if any attachments, especially wives or children that might cause them to hesitate when confronted with the many obstacles that the expedition was certain to confront.

The expedition started off well at sunrise on a clear day that appeared to signal the dawn of a new world to come. But circumstances changed within the first week. In that week, five men had died — Two from hypothermia; three in an unforeseen avalanche just a mile from their destination, destroying their base, pushing them back, and wiping out their route of retreat. Food was scarce, but they were too far along to turn back. There was nothing else to do but soldier on. The wind was a craven force, like a thousand tiny hands slapping you. One man's nose tip turned black. Fingers and toes became small sacrifices to Sir Arthur's quest.

Finally, after much extreme stress and treacherous climbing, a sign appeared. Near the top of the mountain, embedded in the side of a ridge, was a small cabin emitting smoke from its chimney. The remnants of the expedition followed the trail of the smoke and came upon the cabin. Sir Arthur opened the small but heavy wooden door.

Inside the cabin was an old woman who sat by a fireplace. She was thin and frail, and seemed to be covered by one long piece of garment that adhered to her like the furry skin of a bear. Animal hides and pelts covered the walls, and the air inside had a heavy stench of blood and death. The men were all too familiar with those smells. The old woman welcomed them with a simple gesture, holding her hands apart, and (in spite of the stench) they basked in the unusual warmth of the cabin. She opened a door behind one of the animal hides on the wall and showed the men into a room that contained a vast library of forbidden books, lost volumes of knowledge containing the secrets of the universe. The books overflowed the shelves they rested in. Some stood stacked up like pillars against the wall, or lay across the floor on blankets. They were everywhere inside the room, which seemed huge on the inside.

Sir Arthur was glowing inside. Here was the culmination of his life's work. It was just as he had imagined. The secrets were here. He knew it. They must be. The knowledge that he would gain would be of infinite use to mankind, and would help establish his immortality in the historical map of the world. This would be his crowning achievement. There would be no doubt to anyone of his contribution to crown and country.

Once the men were settled, the old woman offered them food from an iron pot held above the fireplace flames by a strong white branch. Why it did not burn was a mystery.

"The books," Sir Arthur asked her, "how did you come by them?"

"The books are immaterial. I keep them to warm the cabin. All of that knowledge has passed."

"But, is it true that in these tomes are the secrets of the universe?"

"Secrets? No. The purpose of knowledge is not a secret. It is a reflex of the heart, of the soul. The secret is a question. You must ask: What is it that is important to me in this brief life?"

With a wooden ladle, she spooned out a thick hot soup and handed each of the explorers a hearty portion. The men settled down on the floor to eat.

"How old are you?" one of the explorers asked.

"I am one hundred and sixteen, the last time I counted. And that was a long time ago." She smiled a crooked smile. There were no teeth visible.

"Lordy," one man exclaimed.

"If you eat, you will know," she said, having no doubt as to their impatience to ask questions. "Talk after."

They were hungry, and so ate voraciously, and in a short time they came to possess the secrets of the universe they all hoped to find.

"The food. Something in the food," Sir Arthur realized. The chemistry in his brain was changing. The knowledge was his, unfolding like a million flowers opening under an incandescent sun. Everything came into focus.

Sir Arthur and the others then realized that it was

useless to go back. No one would believe them. They would most likely be thought mad. The knowledge they had would be dismissed by the ignorant and the superstitious. They would not fit in with society anymore. If there was the remotest chance that everyone understood what they understood, all effort would stop, all conflict, competition, empathy and progress.

They voted to stay in the cabin. The old woman revealed that she was dying, not from any disease, but because it was "her time." She would need someone to carry on for her, to tend to the cabin in case any others in search of knowledge ventured there.

They understood. The men voted unanimously to stay. A storm began to build outside. The wind howled. They sat back and ate some more soup. The old woman gave them fresh hot bread.

"Baking bread, after all, is an easy enough task once you possess the knowledge of the universe," she said, smiling now with a twinkle in her eyes. "But it must be done, like all things, the correct way."

They all sat back and ate their bread.

About the Author

Donald J. Gavron is a writer and graphic designer living with his wife Anna and their two cats in New Jersey. He has written novels, plays, poetry, essays, music reviews and short stories. He is the author of the novel *Glacier: A Tale of Rock 'n' Roll Horror* and the collection *War Wolves and Other Tales of Terror*.

Special thanks to
Bob Helmbrecht and Chris M. Junior